"Terrific…Steve Neil   er
—breathless, on-the-sp...
Weegee crime photo. His is the voice of a generation… gay… ad
only just begun, haltingly and courageously, to speak for themselves.
Come for the page-turning storytelling, stay for the engrossing journey
to a historical era that lies at the roots of modern day liberation. It's a
great book." --Eric A. Gordon, author of *Mark the Music: The Life and
Work of Marc Blitzstein*

"This is a real treat—believable characters who illuminate the dark just
before the dawn of gay liberation. A bonus is the richly detailed
backdrop of Los Angeles in 1956, including political corruption, real
estate scams, Hollywood scandals and organized crime. I'm looking
forward to the sequels." --Peter Cashorali, author of *Gay Fairy and
Folk Tales*

Final Atonement:

Lambda Literary Award Nominee

"Johnson has crafted a literate murder mystery that expands the genre
to include deft commentary on the changing face of urban centers."
                                                        --Publishers Weekly

"One of the most exciting new detectives in years." --John Preston

"Doug Orlando is dedicated, compassionate…appealing.   Johnson
provides an effective and unexpected ending."
                                                        --Los Angeles Times

False Confessions:

The Advocate Bestseller

"Steve Neil Johnson may very well turn out to be our queer Raymond
Chandler… the plot twists are clean and clever… strikingly original…
the best casual reading I've come across yet. Orlando is a great
detective… (builds to) a heart pounding climax."
                                                        --San Francisco Bay Times

Also by Steve Neil Johnson

Final Atonement
A Doug Orlando Mystery

False Confessions
A Doug Orlando Mystery

This Endless Night

For Young Adults:
Raising Kane

For Children:
Everybody Hates Edgar Allan Poe!

Clutching Hand Books edition, August 2012

BOOK I

The L.A. AFTER MIDNIGHT Quartet

THE YELLOW CANARY

STEVE NEIL JOHNSON

CLUTCHING HAND BOOKS

For Lloyd

December, 1956

Chapter 1

He heard the music, wisps of sullen jazz that ached with loneliness, through the open back window as the unmarked patrol car cruised past the bar. No name above the bar door, just a flashing sign in the shape of a caged bird, the glow of neon reflecting yellow ripples in puddles on the gum-scarred sidewalk.

Jim Blake leaned back in the rear seat and told himself to relax. All he had to do was wait for someone to ask him home. How hard could it be? He rested his right hand on the armrest, but his fingers couldn't keep still. He lit a Chesterfield and tossed the match out the window.

The Santa Anas had kicked up that evening, a restless wind scuttling leaves and litter in the gutter, an arid heat that blew through the window and left his face taut and his throat dry.

At the wheel Sergeant Hollings slowed to a stop down the block, nestling the Plymouth Savoy between two parked cars. He glanced over his shoulder at Jim and beamed.

"You ready to get lucky?" Hollings's grin was wide. His bristly dirty blond crew cut and chubby cheeks gave him a boyish look, despite being nearly forty. But Blake had heard around the precinct house that the sergeant's amiable manner belied a stubborn streak and an unerring sense of right and wrong. It had kept him from involvement in the gambling, prostitution, bookmaking, and loan sharking payoff scandals that had almost brought the department down. Hollings wasn't one to ever back off, and that had gotten him in trouble with the brass and left a once promising career floundering in Vice.

Blake wasn't going to let that happen to him.

Riding shotgun, Detective Ryan shifted in the front seat to look back at him. He had a beer keg for a belly, so it wasn't easy. "Let's look you over, you handsome devil." He raised one bushy eyebrow—thick as a mustache—and licked his lips. "Mmmmm, they're going to eat you up." He was enjoying himself too much to even try to wipe the smirk off his face.

"The tie will get them," Hollings commented, playing along and nodding approvingly.

"Yeah, they like bright colors."

Blake felt his cheeks flush and smiled gamely; he had expected a hazing on his first night on the job, and it looked like he was going to get it.

Hollings gave him a wink. "Go get 'em, tiger."

Climbing out of the back seat, Blake hesitated on the sidewalk, pulling on his sport jacket. He was a big man, six foot two, with broad shoulders. He had bought the jacket hurriedly this morning from a men's store on Vermont, and it felt a little tight. It was hard to find jackets off the rack wide enough to accommodate the span of his shoulders, and he hadn't had time for alterations.

"Oh, a little piece of advice," Ryan said, leaning out the window, his expression suddenly serious.

Blake bent toward the front passenger window expectantly.

"If you have to pee, hold your dick tight and your buns tighter."

Shaking his head, Blake forced a grin, and turned down the street. Hollings rolled down his window and stuck his head out. "And if they ask you if you're butch or fem, be sure to tell them you're *fem*." He chortled loudly.

He made his way toward the bar. The sidewalks were nearly empty tonight, but it was early. A few figures, their voices scarcely carrying above the din of traffic, huddled at the corner, and across the way a man exited a tavern, quickly put a hat on his head obscuring his face, and strode rapidly away.

Blake remembered this strip from shore leave during the war, spanning Fifth Street from the downtown central library to the blocks east of Main, where dozens of bars had been plastered with warnings for service members, off-limits to military personnel. The queer run. The streets had been filled with people then, carousing from bar to bar, the all-night coffee shops packed, the parks alive with shifting shadows.

He wondered briefly if he'd made the right choice. He'd also been offered a position in the abortion unit in the homicide division, but had turned it down. Investigating and arresting the victims of botched back-alley abortions— mostly poor women, Negro and Mexican, who didn't have the money to go to the legit physicians who clandestinely performed the procedure—left a sour taste in his mouth.

Maybe this wouldn't be so bad. And in a short while, he would be out of Vice, and he could forget the whole thing. He'd had bad memories before. The war. The war, and other things. No, he'd made the better choice.

The city had changed so much in the last decade that he hardly recognized it upon his arrival last week. The sprawl spread straight to the ocean, and gas rationing and the tops of headlights painted black to protect the city from bombing had given way to a building boom and streets snarled with traffic. The new super highways promised to change all that, and construction was underway all over the city.

Gone were the days when servicemen squeezed two to a bed in overcrowded Ys, and the sound of snoring young men would follow him down to the communal bathroom late at night, where a constant commotion of soldiers coming and going from the ports in Long Beach and San Pedro left the showers busy all night long.

After what had happened here, it was a wonder he could come back. But ten years was a long time, and the city had called to him, first in his nightmares after the war ended and he had returned to Wisconsin. And then, as a gnawing ache that wouldn't let go until he gave his notice to the Milwaukee Police Department and hopped a train to the coast. Yes, a short stint in Vice, and then he would be on to better things. He'd be making $464 a month, one dollar and eighty-two cents per hour after taxes, social security and his contribution to the Widow's Fund were taken out.

And all he had to do was sit at the bar and wait for someone to ask him home.

Though sodomy was a felony that could carry a life sentence in California, none of that would even come into play this evening, he had been assured during training. Section 647 of the Penal Code prohibited soliciting a lewd act. A misdemeanor. A vag-lewd rap.

A sudden gust of dry wind lashed at his face, and he closed his eyes against grit flung upward from the sidewalk. It had always been a dirty city, that hadn't changed. Bits of litter squabbled in the gutter, and the front page of a tattered tabloid darted up and pressed against his ankle, then was swept away. He had seen the scandal sheet earlier that evening: an obviously doctored photo of a city councilman and a sultry blonde B-movie actress cropped in the shape of a heart below the masthead, and the blazing headline proclaiming the two had run off to a secret love nest in Mexico. The whole city was talking about it.

4

brownies. And after she was gone, only his father, always with a bottle; he'd seen him only once upon his return from the war.

When he went back into the barroom, nobody seemed to notice him. He found an empty stool at the far end of the bar near the restroom and sat down. He glanced around casually as he waited for the bartender, who stood at the other end of the counter mixing a drink, to fill his order.

Idly he wondered why his training officers had chosen this particular bar. There were so many along this strip, like the Crown Jewel, with its neon crown above the front door and a strict coat and tie dress code. Maxwell's, near Pershing Square, with its unsavory crowd of self-pitying drunks, shrieking queens and young studs looking for an extra dollar and a place to sleep for the night. And further west, the bars on La Brea, lots of them, and the Pink Poodle on Pico and the Red Raven on Melrose. He'd heard about them all in training. His eyes came to rest on a cage hung above the bar, fluttering with yellow canaries.

"I think it's sad, keeping them like that, stuck in a smoky room. They ought to be out, making things more beautiful in the world."

Blake turned to the speaker, who was sitting on the next stool, noticing him for the first time. He was slight, somewhere in his thirties, nattily dressed in a crisp business suit, his hat lying beside his drink on the bar.

"My name's Jim." Blake offered a firm handshake. The man's eyes brightened and he looked heartbreakingly glad someone was talking to him.

"I'm Charlie."

"Good to meet you, Charlie. Come here often?"

"Not so much. I'm not really a bar person, you see. I work downtown, with the Department of Transportation. Accounting. How about you?"

"I'm new in town," Blake drawled. He remembered what he'd been taught. Be friendly. Engage them in conversation. Gain their confidence. Act like they're the most interesting person in the world. Wait for the pass. Or any attempt at physical contact. "Still looking for work... and a place to stay."

Maybe he had gone too far too fast, because the man swallowed nervously, an expression of longing on his face, as if he wanted to ask Blake home but didn't dare hope, and looked away shyly.

Suddenly he felt sorry for the guy, and wondered if there was someone else, anyone else, he could snare. His eyes began to wander around the room, pausing on a figure who looked like none of the others, standing aloof, leaning in a dim corner by the juke box, the neck of a beer bottle gripped in one hand, his thumbs planted in the pockets of his Levi's. He had on a skin-tight black T-shirt that showed off his narrow waist and muscular chest. His biceps were large and in the dimness Blake spotted a tattoo, something winged, like so many men got in the war. The man was pointedly ignoring everyone in the bar; when his eyes rose and he surveyed his surroundings, it was as though he saw through them. Trade, Blake thought.

A queeny young man who appeared underage kept passing by the man, looking him up and down in undisguised admiration. The boy's shirttails were tied in a knot at his abdomen like a calypso dancer, and his pastel lavender Capri pants could get him arrested on the street.

The man in the black T-shirt continued his pose of utter indifference, but that didn't seem to deter the kid. Through the fog of smoke and milling bar customers, the boy seemed to sense he was being watched and caught Blake looking his way. He tilted his blond head, his eyes narrowing, his mouth forming a frown.

Blake turned away. He didn't want to arrest a kid. Finally the bartender approached, the sleeves of his white dress shirt rolled up, and asked for his order.

"Draft beer would be fine."

"You got it."

The bartender nodded, looking him over in something akin to recognition, and went down the bar. Just then, the kid in the calypso shirt leaned over the bar and spoke to the bartender in a hissing tone, glancing over at Blake. There was a knowing smirk on the young man's face, and Blake couldn't be sure, but he thought he heard the words, "Hollywood Reject."

The bartender didn't seem to need a moment to think about what he'd been told; he went directly to a high shelf behind the bar, rather ceremoniously picked up a glass, and filled it from a tap and set it on the counter before Blake.

Blake couldn't be sure, but he thought a murmur arose from the crowd behind him. To Charlie, the bartender said, rather pointedly, "Can I refresh your drink?" He gazed down at the slight man and subtly—so subtly Blake wouldn't have noticed if he wasn't alert—shook his head at him, warning.

Charlie swallowed and blinked, and looked over at Blake, his eyes suddenly filled with anxiety.

"Oh," he said, in almost a whisper.

Blake peered down at the dry glass in front of him and realized he had been made. Glancing down the bar, he saw all the other glasses were dewy with condensation, taken from a refrigerated box under the bar.

The music on the juke box had stopped and the room was strangely quiet. He looked around and was struck by the realization that everyone in the bar was watching him. Not directly, but out of the corners of their eyes. Waiting. He had seen that look before, like cattle in a slaughterhouse. Several men broke from their friends and headed for the front door, putting their hats on before they got outside.

Charlie swiveled toward him, as if to get off his stool, panic written on his face. He lost his balance and his knee touched Blake's and his right palm landed briefly on Blake's shoulder.

It was enough.

Blake slid his badge and identification onto the bar beside his glass. "You're under arrest," he announced. "I want you to get up quietly and follow me. Do you understand?"

Charlie nodded, but he couldn't seem to stand on his own, and Blake had to grip his arm with both hands to keep him from collapsing.

The bar patrons stared at them, openly now, and there was something in their gaze Blake hadn't seen before, and it wasn't the look of cattle. Suddenly he felt unsafe. The front door appeared way too far to him and the path too crowded, so Blake pulled Charlie past the restroom and to the side door.

The door slammed shut behind them, and when nobody followed, the sense of alarm Blake had felt just moments before quickly dissipated. A stale wind blew down the dark cobblestone alley lined with dumpsters overflowing with garbage. It brought a fetid smell to his nostrils and he could feel slick grease on the stones under his feet. One direction led to utter darkness, the other, the lights and traffic of Fifth Street a dozen or so yards away. A scattering of stars rose overhead.

Charlie collapsed to his knees, clinging to Blake's legs. "Please," he begged. "Please don't do this." He looked up pleadingly.

"It's just a vag-lewd charge," Blake said gruffly. "You pay the fine and you forget it."

"I'll lose my job," he whimpered. "I'll lose everything."

Blake looked toward Fifth helplessly and wished he could just get out of this stinking alley.

The grip of Charlie's hands tightened on his slacks. "I'll have to register for the rest of my life. I won't be able to get another job."

"Not if you plead." He wasn't actually sure of that, but he felt a strange need to reassure this slight little man who had looked at him with such longing minutes before.

"Please," Charlie whispered. He looked up at Blake and light from Fifth Street glinted on his darkened face, catching the tears welling in his eyes.

Blake was getting annoyed now. His training officers would be wondering what was taking him so long, and that sick feeling in his stomach had come back. "Look," he said, shaking his head, "it's just the way things are."

Then Charlie's entire body began to shake. Blake had seen grown men cry before, in the war, in battle, but not like this. His whole body seemed to convulse as he clung to Blake's legs, and a deep sound came from his throat, an eerie wail that floated in the darkness all around them.

"Aw, c'mon. Get up."

Charlie shook his head, silent now, cowering at his feet.

"You knew what you were doing, coming here."

"I'll never come back here again. I promise."

Blake sighed. His mouth was dry and more than anything he needed a cigarette. Reaching into his jacket pocket, he found his Chesterfield pack and lit up. He tossed the match on the ground.

He looked to the far end of the alley, lost in darkness, a darkness pure and deep. He could let him go, he thought. Just let him walk into the night. No one would know. Tell Sergeant Hollings and Detective Ryan there had been no nibbles tonight. Try as he might, he couldn't get any of the fruits to make a pass. He wasn't cut out for it. He must not have whatever they were looking for. Then he could just

11

up and quit this job and forget the whole thing, forget the assessing eyes that lingered, the smoke hanging low, the hot oppressiveness of the bar, forget that ache that had brought him back here in the first place. Just hop the next train to Wisconsin and crawl on his knees to get his old job back.

He sighed again, exhaling a plume of smoke.

Charlie looked up at him hopefully. His voice croaked. "Please?"

Then Blake heard something in the opposite direction, perhaps the backfire of an engine, and he turned his head and saw the unmarked Plymouth crawling down Fifth. It stopped there, at the entrance to the alley, and through the windshield he could see Hollings and Ryan gazing at them and knew his decision had already been made for him.

Billy hurried through the crowd to the front of the bar, jostling elbows and drinks as he went, and pushed open the door into the night air. The moment he was outside he spotted the unmarked police car inching down the street and immediately turned away, quickly untying the knot in the tails of his shirt and tucking them into his pants. With parked cars blocking their view, they wouldn't be able to see his Capri pants or his iffy shoes. And anyway, it looked like they had bigger fish to fry tonight.

Walking fast, he looked back only once, to see the Plymouth come to a halt, the plainclothed officers inside spying down the alley at the far side of the bar.

Billy prided himself at being able to spot a vice cop at thirty yards, not just in the bars, but among the brambles of Griffith Park, by the fountain in Westlake Park, and what was left of the once lush banana tree groves at Pershing Square, which had been largely mowed down to keep

12

undesirables from roaming there at night. Tonight he had been too late, but maybe he could still help that poor guy, whoever he was.

He thought about how attractive the cop had been, and how utterly predictable it all was. And that made him hate them all even more.

After trotting to the end of the block, the dry wind pelting his face, he crossed the street. Everything had been going so well until the cop showed up. He had drunk far more than usual, and that had made him bold. He had almost approached the Man in Black—as he had taken to referring to him—and if this hadn't happened, perhaps he would have. *Finally*.

This had been going on for weeks now. The Man in Black had appeared one night through the smoke of the bar and took his breath away. Billy simply couldn't get him out of his mind. That rugged jaw with the dimple. High cheekbones like an Indian. Those big strong arms. And that little tuft of hair peeking out from the collar of his black T-shirt. Billy could only imagine what it would feel like to touch his chest and run his fingers through that curly hair.

Every night as he fell asleep Billy dreamed of being caressed by him, those arms wrapped around him, holding him tight. And the craziest dream of all, being loved by him. But of course, that was impossible. The Man in Black could never love him. He was hopelessly straight; he had to be. But just to have him, even for a moment, would be the most wonderful thing in the world.

But he couldn't think about that now.

He found a telephone booth outside a cigar shop on the next block and stepped inside, closing the door behind him. He fumbled through his wallet, past the fake I.D.s that established his age at 21, and found the number.

Then his narrow shoulders sagged. No, David Rosen wouldn't be home tonight. It was the second Thursday of the month. He and Paul always went out with that group they belonged to. And then, he remembered where David would be.

It was actually close enough to walk, but he put a dime in the slot and dialed the operator, requesting assistance.

"That number would be MIchigan-1011. I'll connect you," the operator said. After a moment, he heard two rings.

"Biltmore Hotel, good evening," a nasal voice answered.

"Yes, it's important," Billy said. "I need to get a message to someone who is dining there tonight."

Chapter 2

Paul Winters loved their nights out with the girls.

He grinned and winked at David across the table in the Roman Room of the Biltmore Hotel. David took a sip of wine and grinned back at him. Earlier that evening they had picked up Jeannie and Pat, Jeannie sitting across from him in the front seat of his Ford, Pat with David in the back, just like a real double date. They had joined a dozen of their crowd at a long table under wrought iron chandeliers in the Pompeii-inspired sunken dining room and to all intents and purposes they appeared to be a group of married couples sitting side-by-side enjoying a night on the town.

After a toast to Paul for winning another high-profile case and sending a Sunset Strip gangster to life in prison for the killing of a mobster rival, the conversation turned to the *other* headline everybody was talking about. City Councilman Bullock had run off with a starlet named Victoria Lynn and they were reportedly holed up in a love nest in Tijuana.

Paul had seen her in supporting roles in several films—she made at least three a year—and remembered her as a rather stiff blonde beauty. Jeannie, who worked as a make-up artist at Universal and knew all the Hollywood gossip, was holding court.

"It's all a big lie," she announced breathlessly. She had a shiny turned-up little nose, bouncy auburn hair, and a petite frame. Paul had brought her as his date for last year's Christmas party at the D.A.'s Office, and they'd had a big laugh together when everybody said what a great couple they were. "None of it even happened. It *couldn't* have happened."

Parker Huston, two seats down, leaned his chubby torso forward in his seat, his cheeks red from a bit too much to drink, and picked up a steak knife as if readying himself for battle. He rarely suffered being wrong about anything regarding movies or the film industry's social scene. The fact that he worked as a librarian and had no connections whatsoever in Hollywood or to movie stars was beside the point. "Now, dear, how is that possible? It was in *Confidential*, and everybody knows that particular publication has spies everywhere and pays for information."

Pat suddenly came to attention. Nobody—especially Parker—was going to question her girlfriend's credentials on anything Hollywood. Or maybe she was just wrangling for a fight because her high heels fit too tightly. She had looked so miserable in full make-up, a frilly dress and a stole that evening, instead of the jeans and checkered shirt she usually wore for her landscaping business, that Paul felt sorry for her. Even her short hair, usually straight and the color of straw, had a limp wave in it. Everybody had been instructed to make a big fuss about how good she looked, but Paul just saw a boy forced into drag.

David had known Jeannie for quite a while through his political activities and a homophile magazine the two volunteered at, but the girls had become close to them only after a frantic call in the night from Jeannie that Pat had been arrested for masquerading. Paul had quietly advised her attorney that the late nineteenth-century law against wearing the apparel of the opposite sex had been ruled unconstitutional in 1950—despite the fact that vice officers continued to use the statute to arrest men and women whose clothing violated gender norms. Pat had been released the next day.

"Go ahead," Pat urged, eyes shining, "*Tell* them. Tell them about Victoria Lynn."

Jeannie glanced around at the surrounding tables to make sure no one was listening, then bent low in a conspiratorial whisper. "She's *a Lizabeth Scott*, if you know what I mean."

That caused a buzz around the table, and Paul crooked his head at David quizzically.

In response, David grinned and cupped his hand to the side of his cheek and mouthed the word *dyke*.

Then Paul remembered. A nasty exposé in *Confidential* the year before had sent Scott's career into freefall. According to the tabloid, her name and number had been found in the top secret address book of a madam who provided a stable of gorgeous blondes to male—and female—stars.

"That doesn't surprise me," Parker put in, clearly trying to wrestle back control of the conversation. "The most glamorous stars are. Dietrich, Hepburn, Garbo…"

"You think everybody in Hollywood is," David said.

"I think everybody is, because…" Parker replied, refilling his glass, "*everybody is*."

"Victoria Lynn is a goddess" Pat announced. "I love that woman! And she's *one of us*."

"Don't get her started on Victoria Lynn or we'll be here all night," Jeannie warned. Her lower lip pouted. "I'm totally jealous." But Paul noticed the two women were playing footsy all the while under the table.

The maitre d' brought a note to David, who read it silently, frowned, glanced up at Paul, squinted his eyes meaningfully, then rose and excused himself. Paul watched as David made his way across the restaurant, past the standing filigreed candelabra, and into the main lobby. He wondered what he was going to do about David. He was so adorable, and they had such a great time together, but he was way too young for the deputy district attorney. Just out of college, and the seven year age difference was a huge gap in maturity and sensibility. Despite David's rather conservative Jewish upbringing, he could be impulsive—and indiscreet—and that was dangerous in a lot of ways. And the political stuff... just this evening on their way to pick up the girls he'd carped about how wrong it was that they had to pretend to be Normals—as David called them—in order to be welcomed in a group in restaurants and nightclubs.

"But you love going out with Jeannie and Pat!" Paul had pointed out.

"That's not the point!" David had groaned.

Paul took a Marlboro pack from his pocket, lit up, and laid the red-and-white box beside his wine glass.

Pat began to sing melodiously, "You get a lot to like, filter, flavor, flip-top box!" mimicking the commercials on TV.

Parker added his two cents worth, only after making sure the waiter was beyond hearing range.   "Oh, my, my. You *do* know, Mr. Marlboro Man, Mr. Paragon of Masculinity, Mr. Tall-Dark-and-Handsome, Mr. Future District Attorney, back in the twenties *that* particular cigarette was originally marketed to women... and nelly queens. The slogan back then was 'Mild as May!'"

"It's poison," Jeannie said disgustedly. "Did you read that article in *Reader's Digest*?"

"That's what the filter's for," Paul countered, grinning good-naturedly, and tapping an ash into a glass tray at the center of the table. "It's to keep all that muck from going into your lungs."

Parker's eyebrows rose theatrically. "You *do* realize that filter used to have a red band printed around it... to hide *lipstick* stains?"

"Only you would remember that," Paul said. "From experience, no doubt."

"I know what I know, and once a cigarette for nelly queens, always a cigarette for nelly queens, no matter the packaging."

Paul noticed David had returned to the dining room, but was hesitating by the door, signaling to him, and he knew by the expression on his face that something was wrong. Here we go again, he thought.

He put his cigarette pack back in his jacket pocket, and said, "Excuse me."

"If you're planning a jaunt across the street to Pershing Square, count me in!" Parker quipped, taking a sip of wine.

Paul crossed the room quickly and found David in a state of agitation. He'd seen him like this before, and knew what was to come. He couldn't help but be a little annoyed.

"I got a message from Billy," David began excitedly. "I think it sat at the front desk for about an hour because they weren't sure where I was seated. A fellow was arrested at a bar downtown tonight and taken to Lincoln Heights. I just called the jail..."

Paul glanced at his watch wearily. It was getting late and it had been a long exhausting day. All he really wanted to do was go home and climb into bed with David. He felt that spike of resentment he got every time his boyfriend pressured him to get involved in these situations. He couldn't help everybody. It didn't look good at the D.A.'s Office: so far nobody had asked any questions, but he never knew when his interference might get noticed and come back to haunt him. And, anyway, he had only so much influence in cases like this. "What does he want? Legal advice?"

"No," David said. "He's dead."

◇◇◇◇

"Can't you take him down?" Paul asked impatiently. It was hot and stuffy, and the smell of a long succession of prisoners denied shower privileges hung in the air. He turned his face away from the hanging body, as if to provide the dead man some privacy.

Not that that was possible in the narrow cell crowded with the investigative team. The dead man had urinated himself, and a dark patch soiled his groin and ran down his legs to his shiny black shoes, dripping from the tips onto the cement slab below that served as a bed.

After taking his shots, ejecting sizzling flashbulbs from his camera and stuffing them in his pockets, the crime scene photographer had bumped into the corpse as he tried to squeeze around the rest of the team and out into the corridor. Now the body was gently swaying, throwing distorted shadows on the wall. Other than making sure the body was treated respectfully, Paul just wanted to get out of there.

"Don't blow a gasket," Lieutenant Falk responded gruffly. He first glanced over at the medical examiner for permission, awaiting his meek nod, then at his partner, Detective Vincent, who climbed on the slab as Falk went to the door and called down the hall. "Hey, can we get a chair in here?"

A guard scurried down the corridor with a wooden chair and Falk set it on the slab and climbed on top. His partner held the body from behind while Falk wrestled with the end of the brown leather belt lashed around a pipe in the ceiling.

20

Paul stood back, observing as the homicide detectives lowered the body to the slab and laid it there. The victim was a thin male, apparently in his thirties, of average height, dressed in a suit with scrupulously polished black leather shoes. His mouth hung open and Paul could see silver fillings on his upper molars.

"Who is he?"

Falk gazed at the deputy district attorney distastefully a moment before he spoke. He took a toothpick from a case in his breast pocket and slipped it between his lips. He was in his fifties, with a full head of steel-gray hair meticulously slicked back, a craggy alcoholic face flushed with broken capillaries, and gray eyes that stared without wavering. "Charles Turner. Just a poor sap who couldn't face what was coming to him."

Paul wasn't surprised by his unfriendly reception from the homicide detectives. He wasn't particularly popular with the LAPD. One of his first cases at the District Attorney's Office four years ago was prosecuting eight police officers involved in the Bloody Christmas scandal, in which as many as fifty drunken officers had brutally beaten a group of mostly Mexican youths in custody who were rumored to have assaulted two officers. The young men suffered broken noses, perforated kidneys, ruptured bladders, crushed cheekbones. The ensuing scandal had rocked the city and captured headlines for months and threatened the career of Police Chief William Parker, who saw the tide of public opinion turn against him and was forced to suspend 33 officers and transfer 54 more in a show of cleaning up the department.

Of the eight officers actually charged, only one received a sentence of more than a year. But the corrupt foundation of the department had been shaken, and there were those who believed the free pass it had previously received in brutality cases was a thing of the past.

Paul had become a hero to some, especially among the growing minority communities of the city, who had long claimed to be victims of police brutality, and despite his age—just thirty—he was now routinely assigned the highest profile prosecutions. There was little doubt in the minds of his colleagues he was being groomed by the Democratic machine to take over for the District Attorney when he eventually ran for governor.

The police department had a different take on Paul Winters, however, and few officers restrained themselves from letting him know it.

"But he was arrested on a vag-lewd charge, right?" Paul asked. "Why wasn't he brought upstairs?"

This cell was designed for solitary confinement. And quiet reflection for the penitent. No distractions allowed. No windows, no chair to sit on. Just gray cement block walls, the raised cement slab to sleep on, and a porcelain toilet without a seat or lid.

It didn't make any sense. If the victim had been brought in for soliciting, what was he doing on the cell block reserved for gangsters like Mickey Cohen, who had been held here several years before, and found the experience so unbearable that he'd voluntarily transferred to the federal prison on McNeil Island?

Vincent scratched his nose before answering. It was a big nose, his most prominent feature; his hair was thinning and he had the sloped shoulders and stooped posture of a tall man uncomfortable with his height. He watched Paul as if he was memorizing every detail of his face. "There were sweeps of the bars on La Brea tonight. The Fruit Tank was full."

Paul didn't know much about Vincent, other than he had a reputation for racist rants, and there had been complaints about him. He was one of the many older cops who just seemed to be hanging on to get their pensions. He'd been one of the officers transferred after Bloody Christmas, Paul recalled, and that meant he had blood on his hands.

The medical examiner, an odd little man, almost colorless in every category—clothes, skin tone, hair, even personality—crouched over the body and began to do his work. Carefully, he removed the belt from Charles Turner's neck, examined it a moment, then placed it in a bag.

"That's not his belt," Paul said suddenly.

Falk exchanged a glance with Vincent that held for a moment before returning to Paul. He played with the toothpick between his teeth before he answered. "Sure it is," he said. "He doesn't have one on his pants." He pointed at the dead man's waist.

"Black shoes and a brown belt? And look how wide that belt is. It would hardly fit in the loops on his trousers."

"I'm sorry he didn't live up to your fashion sense," Vincent said. "But he was alive when he went into this cell, and there was no one in it but him, as you can see." He raised his arms, apparently to indicate no other prisoners were present. "Therefore, he hung himself with his own belt."

"That belt is scuffed and old. Look at how meticulously he kept his shoes shined."

Falk twitched the toothpick between his teeth. "You're kidding, right? What are you trying to make out of this?"

"What am I... you're not going to investigate, are you?" Paul asked quietly. He was beginning to feel a slow burn in his chest. The victim's belt probably hadn't been long enough—or strong enough—to do the trick, so a more suitable choice had been substituted.

"Investigate what?" Falk looked over at the medical examiner, who had remained silent through the whole conversation, as if he were a diplomat trying to remain neutral. "Suicide, right?"

"All indications are that it was suicide." His voice was so timorous it could only be heard in a room filled with stone silence. "About the belt... I don't know. It does seem a little strange. We'll certainly check it for finger-prints."

"Thanks," Falk said sarcastically. "Now that my prints are all over it."

"It won't be the first time," Paul said.

Falk's gray eyes narrowed. "What are you implying? He died while in police custody. That's bad enough, and when the newspapers get wind of this—and I'm sure you'll be first in line to let them know—we'll never hear the end of it."

"This wasn't a suicide and you know it. You're either lazy, or..."

"Or what? Be careful what you say," Falk warned. "Since no one else was here, it sounds like you're implying he was killed by police officers."

"Take it any way you choose." Paul turned to the medical examiner and said tersely, "Send me your report in the morning," and left the cell without another word to the homicide detectives.

He was angry and frustrated and he didn't know what to do about it. This was dirty, as dirty as any of the corrupt police practices he'd prosecuted these four years, and it never seemed to end. Scandal after scandal, prosecution after prosecution, nothing ever changed. He was half-way down the hall when he felt Falk's presence behind him.

"You know," Falk called after him, "a lot of good men got caught up in the Bloody Christmas thing. A lot of good men."

Paul stopped and felt his shoulders tighten. He recalled that there had been so much blood spilled on the floor in the assault against the youths that officers had slipped and fallen in their frantic attempts to get at them. He stared at his shoes a moment before he turned and looked back at the lieutenant, meeting his unerring gaze. The toothpick twitched spasmodically between Falk's teeth. "Just how good could they have been? I hope you don't have another mess on your hands, Lieutenant Falk."

"No mess. This is clean. As clean as a suicide can be. Case closed."

Paul felt Falk's eyes never leave him as he walked down the corridor to the elevator, punched the button, and waited for the doors to slide open. He didn't believe the forensics results would prove anything. But he didn't care what anybody said. Proof or no proof.

The belt made it murder.

Paul was relieved to see Jeff Dupuis behind the battered booking desk in the front hall.

The young recruit was an attractive Negro in his mid-twenties who was clearly proud of his snappy dark blue uniform and the fact that he was one of the few coloreds in the department, despite pressure from liberal politicians and ministers to hire more. He was taking night school classes to earn his law degree at UCLA, and now and then cornered Paul to ask advice on studying for the bar and opportunities in the District Attorney's Office. But Paul knew there was far more to Jeff Dupuis than initially met the eye.

Sometimes Paul caught Jeff looking at him awfully attentively.

He had learned from David—who always seemed in the know about such things—that Jeff belonged to a secretive club of colored and white men who got together, according to David's breathless account, for wild sex parties and,

25

David added with less interest, helping interracial couples deal with discrimination in employment and housing.

Lately Paul had noticed Jeff's amiable veneer was being worn thin by frequent oblivious comments from white officers around the jail about what a "good nigger" he was, and wondered how long he could keep up the show.

Paul had once come upon Jeff and a couple of the colored janitors taking a smoking break around the side of the building. He had stopped short, unseen, startled by how different Jeff's voice and tone were among other Negroes. He spoke with a weary, disappointed scowl; even his posture was different, the amicable face he shared with his white colleagues taking on the hard edge of the street. It had made Paul wonder later if the friendly rapport between the two of them was real, and if their shared sexual inclinations offered a bridge where race could not. Either way, Paul liked him, and because of that felt concern for the recruit's future. If Jeff thought life would improve for him in the District Attorney's Office once he passed the bar, Paul wasn't so sure. Attitudes weren't all that different there.

"Can I look at the belongings of Charles Turner?"

"Sure, D.D.A. Winters. It's right here." Jeff got up and took a manila envelope from a drab gray file cabinet behind his desk and handed it to Paul.

"How are your studies going?"

Jeff grinned, blinked his eyes sleepily, and seated himself again, picking up a pencil. "Just finished finals, so I have a break for a few weeks before the new quarter. I'm pulling double shifts to make more money."

Paul opened the envelope and shuffled its contents onto the desk. A comb, 53 cents in change, keys on a ring, a tube of ChapStick, a rumpled handkerchief, and a black leather wallet. Picking up the wallet, Paul counted the money inside, 34 dollars, and began thumbing through cards in a narrow pocket. He examined the driver's license of the victim first, then placed it on the desk. After briefly scanning an old selective service card, he set it down, too. It was the third item that interested him.

It was a business card, cream with a bold embossed black scroll. Paul recognized the name on it, and he frowned in disapproval. He had never met him, but had seen him in action in the courtroom and knew his reputation.

Pritchard Sondergaard
Attorney-at-law

There was a phone number and an office address on Sunset. "Do you know if he called a lawyer?"

"He used the phone." Jeff indicated the pay phone down the hall, where a prisoner was now making a call, attended by a uniformed officer. He thought a moment, twiddling his pencil, and nodded to himself, biting his lip. "I think he was holding a card in his hand when he made the call."

Paul was examining the card, wondering uneasily how the victim had come into possession of it, when he heard footsteps clacking on the linoleum down the hall and looked up.

A man was walking—or maybe it was sauntering—toward him, and what struck Paul was his commanding presence, not just because he was tall and broad-shouldered, with a raw handsome face that demanded attention, but because he seemed utterly unaware of the effect he had on others. He was a beautiful sight to see and Paul found it difficult not to stare openly.

"Who is that?"

Jeff tapped his pencil on Charles Turner's driver's license and looked up. "That's the guy who brought him in."

"Of course," Paul said.

Vice hired handsome men to go into bars and wait for someone to make a pass. Paul wondered bitterly if this guy even really understood his looks were being employed to ruin people's lives. It made him angry, because even with what he knew, he was still attracted to the guy, couldn't help himself. Under different circumstances, it easily could have been him in that cell. Paul felt his pulse begin to pound faster and he disliked the man even more. What a pretty little piece of poison coming my way, he thought.

He waved his hand to get the man's attention. "You arrested Charles Turner this evening?"

The man approached, nodded and offered his hand. "Jim Blake. Vice. I'm new. Just moved here from Wisconsin. First night on the job."

Paul shook his hand, which was dry, firm, and powerful. Blake was a good three inches taller, and Paul felt disadvantaged having to look up at him. "Paul Winters. I'm a deputy district attorney."

"Good to meet you." He pulled a cigarette package from his pocket and offered Paul one. When Paul shook his head, Blake slapped the pack against his palm, releasing a cigarette, and lit it. He inhaled slowly. "So, when will I be called to testify?"

"You won't."

Blake tilted his head, a frown forming. "Uh, did he plead already?"

"He's dead," Paul said bluntly. "The officers upstairs say he hung himself."

A crease appeared between Blake's thick black eyebrows, and consternation rippled over his face briefly, then was gone. He had appeared weary to Paul before, but there was something more than a long day weighing him down. The vice cop looked—Paul couldn't grasp what he was sensing at first—yes, he looked like someone had just torn open an old wound, one that had never healed, and he was trying to cover it up. His troubled eyes were a deep blue unlike any Paul had ever seen before, with flecks of coal black.

"But I don't understand..." he sputtered, "it was just a vag-lewd charge."

"Do you even know what that means?" If the defendant could even find a lawyer to represent him—few in Los Angeles would in homosexual solicitation cases—he'd probably be pressured to plead. Going to court was a far too dangerous proposition. It was unlikely a jury would believe the accused over the testimony of a vice cop, regardless of what really happened, and L.A. cops were notorious for lying on the stand to get a conviction. Better to plead and be placed on probation, forbidden to patronize gay bars or associate with homosexuals. Paul knew the police sometimes then visited the defendant's landlord, leading to eviction, and employer, leading to dismissal. Those who worked for the government or companies that had contracts with the feds were especially vulnerable, for they would be deemed security risks, and any entity that didn't fire them would risk losing its security clearance. "When you were with him, did he appear suicidal?"

Blake gripped his chin thoughtfully, five o'clock shadow darkening his jaw. Paul noticed fine black hairs on the back of his hand and around the watch on his wrist. "Maybe... I didn't think so at the time. I mean, he was very upset."

"He asked you for sex?"

There was the slightest hesitation, then, "He touched me inappropriately."

Paul thought of the pale slight man as he gazed at Jim Blake. It wouldn't have been hard for Blake to get anyone in that bar to touch him, and yet, Paul didn't totally believe what the vice recruit said. He hadn't considered it before, but now he wondered if Jim Blake might have had something to do with Turner's death.

"He was in the solitary cell block. Did you bring him there?"

Blake shook his head, and a puzzled expression haunted his face. "My training officers brought him up. Sergeant Hollings and Detective Ryan. But why would he be in solitary? I thought they had..."

"Apparently," Paul said with undisguised skepticism, "it was overcrowded in the tank." In all his years at the D.A.'s Office, he'd never seen overflow detainees sent to other floors. There'd never been an issue stuffing arrestees ten deep if necessary.

Gazing at the vice cop a moment, Paul couldn't be sure if he was telling the truth or covering up for what he or others had done. He seemed genuinely disturbed over the turn of events, but that didn't stop Paul from feeling revulsion towards him. He knew whatever Jim Blake was feeling right now wouldn't stop him from going back to some bar tomorrow night and doing the same thing to someone else.

Blake ran his fingers through his hair, pushing back the black curl that had fallen on his forehead. "Does he... Charlie... Charles Turner... does he have a family? I mean... I guess he wouldn't."

Paul looked away from him in curt dismissal. "No, of course not." He gathered up Turner's belongings and put them back in the manila folder and handed it to Jeff, thanking him. He kept the lawyer's business card, slipping it into his pocket. As he did, he noticed Blake's eyes following it, and there was something in the vice cop's expression—was it recognition?—that made him uneasy.

Without saying goodbye to Blake, without even giving him another glance, Paul walked the long corridor to the jail entrance. He was down the front stairs and on the sidewalk when he heard a voice call out from behind him.

"Hey, wait a minute."

Jim Blake stood at the top of the stairs, the double brass doors swinging shut behind him. On the wall above him the words LOS ANGELES CITY JAIL were carved in stone, flanked by stylized palm tree bas-reliefs. Art Deco lanterns hung on both sides of the doorway, dimly illuminating the stairway. The wind chattered in trees along the parking strip and again a lock of wavy hair fell across the vice cop's forehead.

"Look, I didn't mean for this to happen." There was distress in his eyes. "If there's anything—"

Paul cut him off. "There's nothing you can do. You got what you wanted. You got your first collar, didn't you? Welcome to the LAPD. You have a great career ahead of you."

He turned on his heel and strode to his car parked down the block.

Chapter 3

Originally constructed in 1929 to house 625 prisoners, the Lincoln Heights Jail had been expanded in 1949 to accommodate the burgeoning criminal element in Los Angeles, and as the fifties progressed, some 2,800 inmates crowded the facility. An entire section was dedicated to Chief William Parker's campaign against sexual deviancy, and tonight, the Fruit Tank was filled to capacity.

Dr. Socrates Stone strolled down the cell block with Dr. Joseph Riverton, nodding thoughtfully as he gazed at the black linoleum floor tile marbled with dirty white under their feet, pretending to listen to what his colleague was saying.

But Dr. Stone was simply too excited to pay attention as Riverton droned on about his accomplishments and how as chief psychiatrist for the LAPD Riverton had examined more sexual perverts than anyone in the field. All Stone could think about was how his life would change if he got this job. He could hear his heart pumping in his chest and deeply regretted his palm had been moist when the two men had shaken hands at the beginning of this, his third interview for the position.

A job with the police department would solve all his financial problems. His private practice was struggling, and rent for office space was through the roof. The apartment in Hollywood he shared with his wife and son was just too small. And with a baby on the way... He remembered that house in the Valley that Susan had looked at so longingly, only to have him shake his head that it was too expensive. There was a fenced back yard for when Michael got older, with space for a swing and a sandbox, a big kitchen for Susan, and an extra room that could be used as his study.

"And as you can see," Riverton said, indicating the wire mesh covered bars and the shadowy figures in dim light behind them, "the problem in Los Angeles—as it is in all large cities—is widespread. You have read my book?"

"Of course," Stone said enthusiastically. He had to be diplomatic. Riverton, in his widely read book on the sexual criminal, recommended shock treatment twice weekly. To Stone, this seemed more a punishment than anything, since it merely treated the symptom, and not the underlying disorder. "It is required reading for anyone studying the subject."

Stone himself didn't like the criminalization of a mental condition, and yet, what other tool did society and the psychotherapist have to urge the reluctant homosexual to change? That was what was so extraordinary about his idea. Prison, yes, for the recalcitrant homosexual who repeatedly and unapologetically affronted the strictures of civilization. But for the others, why not give them the choice of therapy and a normal life instead of a degrading jail sentence, an environment that could only reinforce their maladjustment?

The beauty of his idea was that it wouldn't cost the taxpayer a dime; in lieu of prison, the homosexual would pay for his own treatment. This was a vital element of his program, for the homosexual had to take responsibility for his own behavior and stop whining about society's injustices against him.

Once he got his foot in the door with the LAPD, Stone envisioned obtaining contracts with the courts to expand his private practice to accommodate thousands of these homosexuals in group therapy sessions to cure the malignancy, and not just in Los Angeles. Since homosexual activity was illegal in every state in the union—in some states the penalty for sodomy equal to committing murder—it followed that Stone's treatment centers could spread across the country. A psychiatric empire, all of which he would oversee. He would never have to worry about money again, and that house in the Valley would be nothing more than a stepping stone to bigger things.

As they continued down the corridor, a female voice called from a cell close to the end, "If you don't let me out, I'll miss my performance at the Hollywood Bowl tonight!"

"Ah," Riverton said, sighing. "An interesting case."

"My chauffeur is waiting!" the voice shrieked. "Please release me to my adoring public!"

They came to the cell before the last at the end of the block where a very thin Negro woman stood holding the bars. Only it wasn't a woman. It was an effeminate male, his long hair straightened and waved and burnt red, covered by a hairnet. He was wearing a woman's flowered blouse and flowered pants.

"Hello, Alfred," Dr. Stone said pleasantly, pushing his eyeglasses down his nose and peering at the inmate.

Riverton's eyebrows rose in surprise. "So you know of him?"

"Alfred and I are old friends."

Dr. Stone had first met Alfred Washington six years ago as a resident, where the then teenaged patient had been admitted to the psych ward for erratic behavior, pronounced effeminacy, a near obsession with women's apparel, making a spectacle of himself, and getting in a brawl with several white Varsity players for calling him a "dirty nigger queer."

34

Alfred took a step back, his jaw dropping, and said, "Oh." He swallowed and the Adam's apple in his scrawny neck jumped.

Stone remembered the case well. Affecting a superior attitude, the patient had openly proclaimed his homosexuality and insisted that his race was the most beautiful in the world. Further, he cavalierly stated there was nothing wrong with him and he had no interest in therapy. However, after being given 13 electroshock therapy sessions, the patient had become eager to cooperate with the doctors, proclaiming he must have been mad to say such things, and how embarrassed he was by his past behavior. He profusely apologized to the doctors for any trouble he had caused. The patient was soon released.

Later, Dr. Stone had heard that Alfred had again come in conflict with the law, and had returned to the ward for an additional eight shock treatments. And then the doctor had lost contact with the patient.

"You're not really singing at the Bowl tonight, are you, Alfred?"

"No, doctor," he said penitently.

"Have you been soliciting men in parks again?"

"I told that pretty white boy I wasn't interested, but he just wouldn't let up," he said indignantly. "And then he arrested me."

"Do you still have the blackouts?"

"Not so much," Alfred said carefully, avoiding eye contact with the doctor.

That was the problem with shock treatment; much was still unknown about this therapy and why it worked. It seemed successful in treating severe forms of depression, and yet, perhaps because of a lack of uniformity by doctors performing the procedure, also could cause confusion, depression, anxiety, temporary amnesia, blackouts, and brain damage.

35

"Good, I'm glad to hear it."

Riverton gazed at Alfred with a benign expression on his face. "Dr. Stone, in your clinical work, what do you know about lobotomy in helping patients of this sort who are constantly agitated and difficult and always getting into trouble with the law?"

Stone worked to keep the frown from his face. Lobotomy. Another punishment that did nothing to treat the underlying problem. And since recent studies had shown mental patient subjects lobotomized for homosexual and masturbatory inclination actually *increased* such behavior after five years, it could hardly be considered a successful treatment.

"I don't think that's done so much anymore."

"I hope you're going to learn from this, Alfred," Riverton said kindly. The last cell on the block was empty, and they turned around and started back. "Shall I show you the interrogation rooms downstairs before we conclude our tour?"

They went to the elevator down the hall, and when they got inside, Riverton pursed his lips and stroked his odd little mustache that curved upwards at the ends. "You heard, I suppose, about the Hooker woman."

Stone frowned thoughtfully. "Oh, you mean at the American Psychological Association meeting last summer. I didn't know it was a woman. What's she like?"

A grin spread across Dr. Riverton's face. "Tall—easily six feet—and *mannish*."

It was Stone's turn to smile. "And, I would guess, unmarried."

Shaking his head, Riverton turned serious. "No, no, from what I understand, she has a husband. Though"—and here Riverton's grin broke through again—"the marriage is *without issue*." He paused, then added, "There is a joke— apocryphal perhaps—that while doing her research at a drag ball she went to the ladies room and was stopped by a vice cop who thought she was a man."

Stone felt a sense of relief. A woman. A mannish woman. Her findings would easily be dismissed, and her study soon forgotten. So much for the flap at the APA last summer.

On the floor below, they entered a small observation room; a suspect, slouching and sullen, was being interrogated by two officers behind the glass. Stone found the interplay between the policemen and the criminal fascinating, like something he'd seen on *Dragnet*, but noted a number of opportunities were being missed to break the suspect down. He wondered if Los Angeles police officers studied psychology. It struck him how valuable his assistance could be to the interrogating officers.

After watching for a while, Riverton turned to him and said, "Well, I think you'll fit right in, Socrates. The job is yours, if you're interested." He held out his hand.

Stone quickly wiped his palm on his thigh and took Riverton's hand, smiling gratefully. "Thank you, sir. You won't regret it."

"Welcome aboard."

As Riverton began to lead him out of the room, Stone hesitated, then turned back to the glass. "Wait a moment, if you don't mind," he said. "This interests me."

Paul pulled his Ford Fairlane to the curb in front of his apartment building on San Vicente Boulevard in Brentwood and noticed the light in his second story bedroom window was on. David would be there, waiting for him. They had planned to spend the night together, and he had looked forward to it, so why did he feel so ambivalent now? Maybe it was just exhaustion, but again he had to ask himself just exactly what he was doing in this relationship. He cared about David—he cared a lot—but they were so different, and he wasn't sure how fair it was to keep things going if it could never be more than a fling. He knew that David was already more involved than he was, and David was too nice a guy to hurt like that.

He got out of the car and headed for the front door. Birds of Paradise reached high on both sides of the stairs and bougainvillea crept around the first floor windows.

The Red Car tracks that had once run down the middle of the boulevard had been pulled up and now the median was grassy and lined with young twisting coral trees that in spring would offer bright red blossoms. Paul wouldn't miss the clanging, creaking trains that ran from downtown straight to the ocean, and even though smog lay yellow and sticky over the city during the summer and traffic was getting worse every year, at least the new super highways promised to alleviate the latter. Already the Pasadena parkway was complete and work had begun on a freeway from downtown to San Pedro. Soon the city would be crisscrossed with "miracle motorways," as they had been called in earlier days. Gone would be the corruption of the Southern Pacific Railroad's stranglehold on state and city governments, with its payoffs and election manipulation. Even the Red Cars had been one of their subsidiaries. The advent of the automobile was a crushing defeat for the railroad barons who had controlled the country in the earlier part of the century. And with cheap gas, soon everybody would have a car in their garage.

Shutting the front door, Paul passed through the living room and stood a moment at the bedroom doorway loosening his tie.

Even though the bedside table lamp was on, David lay asleep in bed, a sheet only partially covering his naked body. He had curly dark hair, a large nose that made him more handsome rather than less, and full lips that Paul found provocative in that they seemed to demand to be kissed. Paul felt a rush of affection for him, and brushed aside all his concerns. He seemed to do that a lot when they were together.

As Paul began to undress, his eyes fell on his reflection in the bureau mirror. He had a strong face with moist dark brown eyes, meticulously barbered brown hair and an aquiline nose. David had once commented with an amused curve on his lip that no one looked more comfortable in a suit. When Paul tossed his jacket and slacks on a chair by the bed, David opened his eyes and stretched his arms.

"You took forever," he said groggily, glancing at the clock and rubbing his squinting eyes. "What happened?"

"You already know about as much as I do. A man who was arrested for soliciting in a bar downtown was found hanging in his cell."

"Did he kill himself?"

"No." Something else had happened in that cell, he was sure, but he also knew things like this happened every day that were never accounted for. Little deaths that mattered to nobody.

"Then what happened?"

"I don't know. Let's go to bed."

"Did they kill him?" David demanded. Now he was sitting up in bed, alert. This was exactly what Paul didn't like, and he was reminded why he had reservations about their relationship. "Did the police kill him?"

"Since there was no one else in the cell, that seems likely." Paul sighed, stripping down naked. He ran his hand through the fine hair on his chest.

"We should do something. We should protest."

"You know that isn't possible."

"What about the Negroes? They're doing it."

He went to the bureau and began to lay out his clothes for tomorrow. "Just stop it, David. I'm tired."

The whole idea was ridiculous. How could you protest like the colored? It would be tantamount to admitting one's homosexuality. If he did, Paul knew he'd immediately be dismissed from his job as a Deputy D.A., his dream of ever becoming the District Attorney of Los Angeles would be dashed, and possibly he would be disbarred. Anybody who worked for the government who publicly acknowledged their homosexuality would be fired—and anyone who worked for a company that had contracts with the government. Even hiding who you were didn't keep you safe. Any third-party accusation of homosexuality would lead to dismissal. It had already happened all over the country—since the late forties thousands had been let go—when federal anti-communist investigations led to wholesale purges of homosexuals as security risks. More homosexuals had been let go than communists. Now police departments had begun to feed the federal government arrest records of homosexuals, whose employers were visited by government agents and warned to terminate them or risk losing their government clearances and contracts.

As he hung his jacket in the closet and laid his slacks over a hanger, he felt the business card in a pocket. "David, what do you know about Pritchard Sondergaard?"

"Pritchard Sondergaard?" He sounded a little surprised. "He's an evil little queen who dresses like Sydney Greenstreet and exploits us to get rich. They say he's the secret owner of a gay bar downtown, that he owns lots of property around there. He tells all his clients arrested for solicitation to plead so he doesn't have to bother to go to court and then charges them a year's wages. Why?"

Paul knew that wasn't the worst legal advice a defendant in that situation could receive considering the alternative. "Oh, nothing."

David remained silent for a minute, shifting on the bed to a lying position, cupping his chin in his hand, his elbow in the pillow, his mischievous brown eyes observing Paul as he went about his preparations.

"Why do you lay your clothes out like that every night?" With an amused expression on his face, David watched Paul as he reached in a drawer and pulled out a roll of socks. "Too sleepy to turn on the lights in the morning?"

Paul grinned despite himself—his annoyance gone as quickly as it had come—and held the ball of socks in his hand warningly. "Are you gonna shut up?" His eyes glittered.

"Afraid the electric company will turn off the power and you won't be able to find your undies?"

Paul jumped on the bed and playfully pinned both of David's arms down with one hand. David didn't exactly fight back. "Is this what it's going to take to shut you up?" He held up the rolled socks with gleeful menace.

"I prefer your jock strap after a sweaty workout."

"That can be arranged."

Paul felt himself go hard and despite his exhaustion he knew he wasn't going to be able to stop himself. David did that to him. Paul tossed the socks in the air and peeled back the sheet. He ran his hand down David's chest, admiring his white skin, then pulled him up, a bit roughly and tightly, into his arms and kissed him firmly. He found himself exploring David's mouth and reached down and gently began to spread his legs.

"No, cap'n, please," David squeaked, a little breathless, in a British accent, "I ain't never been buggered before, golly I haven't!"

"Okay, that does it, I'm going for the sock!" Paul dove for the ball of socks on the other side of the bed and proceeded to try to cram it in David's mouth, who started giggling and wrestling for the socks. Soon they were rolling across the sheets and collapsed in each other's arms, exhausted and covered in a sheen of sweat. They looked into each other's eyes for a long time, breathing hard and in unison, not saying anything.

"I love you," David whispered, stroking Paul's cheek.

In response Paul kissed him, but it wasn't enough. At first maybe it was, but not now. He knew David was waiting.

David almost winced, glancing away from him, then gazed directly into his eyes. "You never say it, you know."

"I *have*."

"Yeah, like maybe once. In the heights of orgasm. That doesn't count."

Paul sighed and shrugged. "I don't like it when you pressure me. You know how I feel about you."

"Yeah, you let me know without saying a word," David muttered. He abruptly pulled away and reached over and switched off the light. He turned away, but let Paul hold him, and their bodies felt good together, wrapped as one.

Soon Paul felt David fall asleep in his arms, his body going lax, the gentle wheeze of his breath soothing in the night, and he asked himself again what he was going to do about this relationship. But as he fell asleep himself, he found he wasn't thinking of David anymore. Of all the things that had happened that day, from winning his case against a slick racketeer that was sure to pay off big in his profession, to the puzzling death of a man in a solitary jail cell, what he remembered most were the haunted eyes of a vice cop he didn't like very much named Jim Blake.

◇◇◇

Something that Dr. Riverton mentioned had begun to nag at Socrates Stone and he stopped by his office in Hollywood that evening before going home. He switched on the television set in his waiting room before proceeding into his inner office. He liked to have noise in the background when reading, needed it in fact. Something about the silence of a room left him deeply troubled.

He sat behind his desk and rifled through some newsletters that he had stuffed in a drawer and hadn't had a chance to look at. He found what he wanted, leaned back in his swivel chair, and began to read. It was an article about the Hooker woman and her presentation before the American Psychological Association that summer.

Dr. Evelyn Hooker was a UCLA professor and social psychologist who had done something no therapist had ever considered doing before. Rather than basing her conclusions about homosexuality on individuals found in therapy or mental institutions, she based her study on functioning homosexuals. Compared against a control group of Los Angeles policemen and firefighters, the homosexuals were just as well—actually slightly better—adjusted mentally. Her finding that homosexuality was a sexual pattern "within the normal range, psychologically" had created a firestorm at the APA meeting.

Stone frowned, listening for a moment to the lively strains of a musical variety show coming from the waiting room. What people like Hooker didn't understand was that conformity—and that included sexual conformity, in fact, *especially* sexual conformity—was the hallmark of maturity and mental health, and without it, society would be plunged into chaos.

She certainly wasn't doing the homosexual any favors, Stone thought savagely, stuffing the newsletter back in a drawer; far too often in his own practice he had seen patients resistant to becoming normal and taking on the natural male role of husband and father.

Dr. Stone knew only too well that the homosexual was lazy and self-indulgent, and sly, too, easily slipping back into old patterns even after therapy, and now they were being given *carte blanche* to continue a destructive way of life. Destructive, not just to the individual, but to society itself, to the future stability of the country. All you had to do was read the papers to see the congressional committees formed to stop the security threat posed by these people.

This was not the first time he had heard of such madness. He remembered back in his undergraduate days coming across a 1914 book in the university library by a German physician, a Magnus Hirschfeld, who argued that homosexuality was an innate and unchangeable drive, nothing to be ashamed of, and society's attitude was the problem. Dr. Hirschfeld recommended a treatment of building self-esteem in the patient, discussing famous homosexuals throughout history and the wide extent of the condition past and present. He urged all attempts at intercourse with the opposite sex to cease, and all drugs including morphine prescribed by previous psycho-therapists be immediately discontinued. He suggested reading books on the subject such as the dialogues of Plato and associating with other homosexuals of high moral and intellectual character.

Rising from his chair, Stone turned off the light in his office and went into his waiting room. What he saw on the television filled him with further dismay. A syndicated variety show had just come back from a commercial break and its star was talking to the audience before his next number. Stone adjusted the rabbit ears to get better reception and watched gravely.

This was part of the problem, too, and it was coming into everybody's homes.

It was impossible to assess whether this young entertainer, whose name was Liberace, was in fact a homosexual or not—he certainly had legions of female fans, both young and old who adored him—but his effeminate mannerisms and festive apparel, broadcast across the nation, could only lead to confusion in young boys and a continued erosion of the defined roles between the male and the female.

Dr. Stone had recently read in a psychiatric journal a startling argument by a therapist who posited the disturbing possibility that the rise in sexual perversion seen in recent years was only the tip of the iceberg, that the Second World War had inadvertently created an environment favorable to the maladjustment: with the adult males of the country absent for long stretches and young boys coddled by their mothers lonely for male love. It was a recipe for disaster.

He thought of his own son Michael, just two years old, and what this kind of influence would have on him. But, of course, it was impossible that his son could turn out that way. He was a strapping boy, a real boy. There was nothing to worry about. You could tell by that age.

Stone turned off the TV set, watching as the picture of the tuxedo-clad entertainer—who ingratiatingly grinned at the camera while dancing his bejeweled fingers across the piano keys—imploded into a tiny star at the center of the screen before going out.

He locked up his office and went home.

Chapter 4

When Paul spotted him in a parked car across Sunset the next morning, his first reaction was surprise. And then, with the realization that this couldn't be a coincidence, unease flashing into anger. He felt that rush of adrenalin he'd experienced the night before as he strode heedlessly across the street, sidestepping oncoming traffic, and approached the gray Hudson Hornet sitting in front of a chrome-plated diner. The Santa Anas had died down during the night, and the day had broken crisp, bright and still, the sky a clean brittle blue.

Paul loomed in the street in front of the driver's window, glowering. He knew a confrontation was a mistake when he couldn't predict the outcome, like asking a question in court he didn't know the answer to, and yet he couldn't stop himself. Inside the car, Jim Blake looked at him without saying anything.

"Why are you following me?" Paul demanded.

Rolling down the window, Blake calmly replied, "I'm not."

"You just happened to show up where I'm going this morning?"

"I knew where you were going. I saw the business card you put in your pocket last night. His office opens in—" he looked at his wristwatch "—five minutes."

"The problem with that is you didn't see what was written on the card because I slipped it into my pocket too

46

quickly. And that means the only way you could have known where I was going would be by tailing me." With a touch of fear it dawned on him that the vice cop might not have followed him from the District Attorney's Office; he could have been shadowing him from his apartment in Brentwood. He remembered with sharp regret that he and David had left the apartment together, and promised himself that he would never be so careless again.

Blake hesitated a moment before responding. His eyes, so striking the night before, were somewhat muted in the morning sunlight. They drifted away, then came back to rest on Paul's irate face. "I gave it to him," he said finally.

Paul blinked. "You…"

He let out a long sigh, his hands loosely clasping the steering wheel. "My training officers gave me a stack of that lawyer's business cards. I was supposed to hand them out when I made an arrest."

Paul took a moment to process that information. "Hollings and Ryan gave you business cards for a lawyer to hand out…" Then he shook his head and chuckled with disgust. "I love it. Great. Sounds ethical." He noticed his right shoe unconsciously tapping wrathfully on the pavement, as if it belonged to someone else. Payoffs and kick-backs were hardly unheard of in the LAPD, but this was a new low. He recalled the reputation of the lawyer in question and had an idea of what had been going on, and it made him sick. "Okay, I get it now. So what are you doing here?"

"I want to go in with you."

Again Paul had to ask himself just how much the vice cop knew about Charles Turner's murder and if he had been involved. The notion that Jim Blake's interest in the case might stem from a desire to keep tabs on Paul and make sure he failed to discover the truth didn't seem an idle one. He wondered if Blake was taking his marching orders from Hollings and Ryan—or even more disturbing, the homicide detectives Falk and Vincent.

"Now why would I let you do that?"

Again Paul saw that flicker of pain he had seen the night before in Blake's eyes, the wound he covered so quickly.

"Look, he killed himself because of me. You don't have to tell me. I know what I did."

He said it with such sincerity that Paul believed in his honesty despite his suspicion and all his reservations about the man. As Paul gazed at his striking features, the sharp-cut thick eyebrows, black as the hair on his head, the strong nose, the five o'clock shadow that didn't go away even after a morning shave, his heartbeat finally began to slow.

Leaning back in the car seat, a shadow fell across Blake's face. "I knew someone a long time ago who killed himself. I want to make this right. I just don't understand how this lawyer has anything to do with it."

Paul glanced through the traffic at the white stucco Spanish-style office building across the street. He was going to have to make a decision, but he didn't know how far he should trust this vice officer. Then it occurred to him that Blake might have information he could use.

"How was Charles Turner dressed last night?"

Appearing surprised by the question, Blake tilted his head at him. "He was well dressed, in a business suit."

"Do you remember what his belt looked like?"

He leaned forward in the window, squinting in the sunlight. "No. Why would that be important?"

"He was found alone in his cell, hanging from a thick, scuffed brown belt, but his shoes were black and shiny."

Blake seemed to let the implications sink in. "You think he was murdered in police custody?"

"I know he was."

"What's this lawyer got to do with it?"

"That's what I want to find out."

48

Across the street Paul spotted a short and portly man in a white linen suit climbing the steps into the office building. He wore a white fedora with a black band and his shoulders were covered by a cape.

"That's him. Pritchard Sondergaard." He knew the lawyer had a dubious reputation. He was at once well-liked and generous, known for representing poor clients for free, but also notorious for gouging others and retaliating viciously when crossed. He was one of the very few lawyers in town who would represent homosexuals in sex arrests—an endeavor far too sordid for most litigators' taste—and yet he was known to dine with the mayor at Chasen's and was rumored to be the lawyer studio moguls called—often on his home phone in the middle of the night—when stars were caught in sex scandals that needed to be hushed up. Paul had seen his antics in court, using humor and charm to win over juries and judges. He was a showman, but there were those who questioned whether he put his clients or his own interests first. Paul tightened his fingers around the business card and wondered exactly how much of an advocate Sondergaard had been for Charles Turner.

Blake opened his car door and joined Paul on the street. "Are we going or not?"

Without answering, Paul made his way across Sunset dodging traffic with Blake at his side.

On the second floor, they entered through a door with a pebbled glass panel into a spacious office decorated in Bauhaus Modern. A secretary with blood-red hair and blood-red lipstick on her tight little mouth stood behind her desk staring at them as they came in. She must have been in her late thirties, with a seen-it-all big-city-girl expression on her face. Her eyes matched her steel-blue two-piece suit, a severely contoured jacket with a wasp-waist that flared to accommodate generous hips, the skirt tapering gracefully to below the knees.

"Yes?" She produced a mechanical smile.

"I'm Deputy District Attorney Paul Winters and this is Officer Jim Blake from LAPD Vice to see Mr. Sondergaard."

"He's having his breakfast." She angled her head. "And nobody disturbs him when he's having his breakfast."

She sat demurely in her chair, and slipped an appointment book from a drawer. Her desk had a plate glass top supported by chrome tubing with symmetrical drawers suspended weightlessly on both sides. Across the room a couch appeared to be made of giant multi-colored marshmallows.

"Unfortunately," she said, sliding a lacquered red nail down a page of the appointment book, "he's very busy today."

Paul took a step closer, and noticed the late morning was blocked out for the lawyer to attend a city council meeting. She caught his eye, placed a porcelain hand over the page, and said wryly, "Now you're being a bad boy, and I was trying to help you."

"Miss?"

"Miss Silvia Havenford."

There was a scalloped silver tray on the desk for business cards. Paul placed the card he had gotten from the dead man's wallet on it and said, "Miss Havenford, give this to him. He'll see us."

She gazed at the card a moment, then back at Paul. "You want to get me in trouble, don't you?"

Miss Havenford rose from her desk with the tray and went to the door behind her, tapped lightly, turned and said reproachfully, "You get what you want, then I have to put up with him being cranky for the rest of the day, and you're long gone," then stepped inside and closed the door after her. She wasn't away more than a moment.

She came out and held the door open for them, a glacial smile on her blood-red lips that held no malice. "Mr. Sondergaard will see you now." She let them pass, then closed the door behind them.

"Gentlemen, gentlemen, gentlemen, what can I do for you today? I have to apologize, I just got in this morning, and I'm just about to have my breakfast."

Pritchard Sondergaard, all five-feet-four of him, sat behind a Bauhaus Modern desk with a tea setting in front of him. In his early forties, he had a potato for a face, with bristly black eyebrows, milk chocolate eyes that peered rather than gazed, and a bald patch at the crown of his head. A carnation, small and tight and the color of his secretary's lips perched in his lapel. His cape was tucked on the back of his swivel chair, his large-brimmed fedora on the desk under an arched-stem reading lamp with a shade like a coolie hat.

"Deputy District Attorney Paul Winters," Paul introduced himself, "and this is Jim Blake, LAPD Vice."

"I know who you are, my secretary just told me." He picked up the fedora, and without rising tossed it in the direction of a coat rack that looked like an electrical tower from an Erector Set. It landed on a prong, wobbled, then settled down.

"Do sit down," Sondergaard said, gesturing animatedly with his stubby hands at two chairs facing his desk. "There, Officer Blake," he pointed to one, "and there, Mr. Winters," he pointed to the other, his eyes locking on Paul. "I do believe I've seen you in the courthouse, but I don't think we've ever met formally."

Blake sank into comfortable plush black leather—the chair's back and armrests were like curved bloated Tootsie Rolls. Paul was less fortunate, easing into what appeared to be an oversized half coconut rind tilted backward and resting on metal legs as narrow as TV antennas. If he didn't sit awkwardly on the edge of the seat, he found himself falling back and being almost swallowed in the deep shell. Paul noted that it was difficult to be taken seriously in a chair like this and realized Sondergaard was too clever a litigator not to be aware of the disadvantage it put him in.

Sondergaard indicated the tea setting before him. "I come from a vaudeville family. Traveled since the day I was born. All over the country, Europe too. Spent part of my childhood in England. Worst cooks in the world. For their greasy fish and chips alone they deserved the Blitz. But I became accustomed to their scones with clotted cream and I haven't been able to break myself of the habit since. Jam alone just won't do."

He went to a credenza along the wall and got two more tea cups and brought them to the desk. "I have it imported from Devonshire. You can't find it in the stores. It has no shelf life."

"No tea for me, thank you," Paul said.

"No thanks," Blake said.

With his back to them as he hovered over the tea set, Sondergaard seemed to go rigid for a moment, then, as if not hearing them, poured tea into three cups from a steaming pot.

He held out cups to Paul and Blake, waiting for them to take them, his voice like polished steel. "Indulge me."

So this is how it's going to be, Paul thought. "You like it your way, don't you?" he commented amiably.

"Always."

Paul took the cup then set it on a table beside his chair and never looked at it again.

Back behind his desk, Sondergaard smiled and said, "I can't be eating in front of you, now can I? Please." He indicated they should take a scone, but neither did. Then he spread clotted cream from a small bowl on a scone and took a bite. "Now, gentlemen, what can I do for you?"

"Did you receive a call last night from Lincoln Heights Jail from a man named Charles Turner requesting representation?"

Sondergaard took another bite, and this time he didn't bother closing his mouth when he chewed. "Can I ask why you're asking?"

"Yes, and we can do a little dance if you'd like, or you can answer my question."

"The answer to your question is that yes, I did receive a call from Mr. Turner at the city jail, and yes, I did agree to represent him at his arraignment. I also told him I had other business this morning and wouldn't be able to get to him until this afternoon."

"Well, you can scratch him off your calendar. Charles Turner died last night in police custody."

Shaking his head ruefully, Sondergaard let out a long sigh. "That is very sad, very sad indeed." He picked up his cup, blew away the steam, and began to sip.

"That's all you have to say."

"What more do you want me to say? He called asking me to represent him on a soliciting charge. I didn't know the man."

"You could have asked how he died. He didn't say anything else to you?"

Glancing down at his teacup a moment before answering, Sondergaard said, his tone pleasant, "And what else would he possibly say?"

"That's what I'm asking. Interesting that he knew to call you."

"Not so interesting. I'm rather well known in that area of the law." He pushed back his chair, said, "Excuse me, gentlemen," and went out to speak to his secretary for a moment, then returned.

"I said it was interesting," Paul continued, when Sondergaard had settled back in his chair, "because he had your card. Given to him by vice officers."

"Mr. Winters, listen to yourself. Are you suggesting these people don't have a right to representation?"

"I'm suggesting you make a pretty penny defending them... and some of that filters back to the arresting officers who gave them your card in the first place."

Looking aghast, Sondergaard dramatically clutched his hand to his chest, as if he were having a heart attack. "Graft? In Los Angeles? Surely you jest, my friend."

"How much do you charge them?" Blake asked suddenly, leaning back in his chair, his first contribution to the conversation.

Sondergaard looked him up and down with his peering eyes before answering, seeming to notice him for the first time. There was something about his expression, a mix of appreciation and contempt, that reminded Paul of the rumors he'd heard about the flamboyant lawyer and where his bedroom interests lay.

"A few thou. Two or three."

Blake sat up in his chair and whistled.

Sondergaard's eyes narrowed and his mouth tightened. "And what price do they pay because of *you,* Mr. Vice Cop? And *you,* Mr. Prosecutor? You seem to forget, they come to me because the LAPD arrests them and the District Attorney's Office prosecutes them." He gripped his hands on the edge of his desk, as if about to get up. "Now, gentlemen, I have appointments to keep. If you have nothing else..."

"Only that your client was murdered," Paul said. "Just in case you wanted to know."

The telephone rang and Sondergaard picked it up. "Yes… yes… yes. Yes, they're here." For a moment his face appeared to contain no expression at all. "So that is the official assessment of the situation? Very good. Thank you, Lieutenant Falk." He hung up the phone. "You have a vivid imagination, D.D.A. Winters. The police report says Charles Turner died by his own hand."

Paul smiled. "Funny thing. I didn't tell you Lieutenant Falk was assigned the Turner case. Isn't it interesting you knew who to contact?"

"It's called having an efficient secretary, Mr. Winters. Perhaps I'll lend her to you sometime. I asked Miss Havenford to put in a call to the Lincoln Heights Jail and ask for the detective in charge of the case and get him on the phone. Any other questions?"

"What's on the agenda at the council meeting?"

The peering eyes blinked. "The city council?"

"I believe your efficient secretary blocked out a couple of hours on your appointment book for you to attend."

Sondergaard hesitated. "I'm having lunch at the Cocoanut Grove with a few of the councilmen, if that's what you mean. Anything else?"

"That's all." Paul climbed from his seat with as much dignity as he could muster. Blake got up with considerably less effort and joined him at the door. "Oh, one other thing," Paul said as he opened it. "Tell the councilmen hello when you see them this afternoon."

"I will." Sondergaard's face was impassive but his milk chocolate eyes were cold and hostile. "And I'll say hello for you to your boss, the District Attorney." His lips parted briefly in a triumphant smile. "He'll be there, too."

"Like I said, you like it your way."

"Always."

◇◇◇

In the outer office, Paul sidled up to Miss Havenford's desk.

"Any chance there might be room for us later in the day? Say at three or four."

She ran her fingers down a page in the appointment book. Paul leaned over her and she gave him a raking glance.

"Step back D.D.A. Winters or get spanked."

"You caught me." He smiled at her. "Come to think of it, maybe an appointment later today wouldn't work out after all."

Her lips tightened into a hard little blood-red wound. "I agree, it wouldn't." She slapped the book shut. "Goodbye, and have a pleasant day. If you could be so good, next time, to call first?"

In the hallway outside the office, Blake asked, "What was that all about?"

"There was no time blocked out this afternoon for Charles Turner's arraignment."

"So?"

"It means Sondergaard knew he was dead all along."

Weaving between oncoming traffic on Sunset, they crossed to the Hudson Hornet parked in front of the chrome-plated diner and when he slid behind the wheel Blake was a little surprised that Paul Winters got in the passenger side without any apparent hesitation. He wasn't sure if the deputy district attorney had changed his mind about him; at least he didn't seem actively hostile anymore. Maybe they were a team. Blake had felt a strange curiosity about him since they'd met the night before, and he didn't know what to make of it. He only knew he wasn't going to let go of this case. He owed Charles Turner at least that much.

After learning of Turner's apparent suicide the night before, Blake hadn't slept well. Memories of Jack Spencer and the way he died came back to haunt him as they hadn't since just after the war, and with them the guilt and feelings of betrayal and all the questions that would never be answered. He knew now he never should have come back to L.A. It was foolish to have even considered it. Maybe it was the way Charles Turner had died, so alone, that brought it all back. That, and the not knowing, the not knowing what goes through a man's head in the moments before he dies.

Blake pulled his cigarette package from his jacket and rattled it, peering inside. "I'm all out." He crumpled the pack and shoved it back in his pocket.

"Have one of mine." Paul offered him his Marlboro box, shuffling it to free a cigarette. There was something about the prosecutor that left Blake feeling flustered, like a teenager on a first date. He hadn't noticed before, but the deputy district attorney was a good looking guy, with an athletic build and attractive features and intelligent, thoughtful brown eyes; but it was his professional manner, as if all the rough edges that Blake disliked in himself had been smoothed down, that he admired most. He guessed getting an education, something he had too little of, made the difference. But he had always been too restless to last long in a classroom. Maybe that was why he'd had so many intrusive thoughts about Paul Winters since they'd met, that he felt somewhat out-gunned by the man sitting next to him.

"Thanks."

Paul lit his own, and with what was left of the flame, held it under Blake's, who took a deep draw until the end of the cigarette glowed red. Waving out the match, Paul rolled down his window and tossed it into the gutter.

"I don't like any of this." Paul shook his head grimly. "Sondergaard has a kick-back deal with Hollings and Ryan. They arrest suspects and slip them his business card for a piece of his fee."

"Just Ryan," Blake said slowly. "It was Ryan who actually gave me the cards, now that I think about it. I'm pretty sure Hollings is clean. He's got a reputation for it in the department and it's kept him down. You mentioned Turner's arraignment wasn't listed in the appointment book—you think somebody called Sondergaard earlier and told him he was dead?"

"Maybe. But it wasn't crossed out, it was never there in the first place." Paul frowned thoughtfully. "What if he already knew what was going to happen to Charles Turner once he got to the jail? Could this have been all planned beforehand? Maybe they wanted to have Turner out of the picture. You arrest him for solicitation, then they fake his suicide once he's in custody."

"I don't see how that's possible."

"They didn't tell you to go after a specific person? Show you a photo? Maybe describe who you should go after by the way he was dressed?"

Shaking his head, Blake said, "No. I mean, I was told to sit beside lonely guys drinking by themselves and strike up a conversation. But other than that..."

"So it was completely random?"

Blake thought a moment. He rolled down his window and a cool breeze flowed through the car. He flicked a nugget of ash onto the street. "It would have to be. There was no way they could know—no way I even knew—who I was going to sit next to."

Paul was silent a few seconds. "Then it wasn't who he was that was important to them. That means something happened to him after he was arrested that made him a threat."

Blake wondered what that could possibly be. "Enough to kill him?" he asked doubtfully. Could Charles Turner have seen something? It didn't seem likely. And if he had seen something that required killing him, why hadn't others seen the same thing and posed the same threat?

"Run me through everything that happened once you arrested him."

"It was pretty straightforward." Blake swallowed and took another drag. The memories tugged at him, as they had the night before. "He was quiet in the car when we brought him in." Blake had sat next to him in the back seat, a broken down man who didn't say a word, head hanging low, forlornly staring at his own feet. He kept thinking of those pleading hands clinging to his legs in the alley, and the darkness at the other end, the darkness that seemed to go on forever. "We brought him to the booking desk. That colored guy was behind the desk."

"Jeff Dupuis."

"Yeah. And then Hollings and Ryan accompanied him upstairs with a guard."

"To solitary?"

Shaking his head again, Blake told him, "No, he was going to the Fruit Tank. I remember because the colored guy—Jeff Dupuis—assigned him a cell. Then they told me I could go take a coffee break."

"They claim the tank was full, so he was put on the solitary block…" Paul mused. "Do you remember which cell number he was assigned in the tank?"

"Yeah. Cell fifty-four."

"Something happened in that cell that made somebody very afraid…"

"…and so they moved him to solitary," Blake continued the thought. "And killed him."

Paul glanced out the window at the chrome-plated diner, then back at Blake. "Let me go make a call."

◇◇◇

Paul dropped a coin in the slot and dialed.

"Lincoln Heights Jail."

"Jeff, it's Paul Winters here. How are you?"

"Sleepy, but it's better than cramming for finals."

"Look, I need a little information, and if you could keep it under wraps, I'd appreciate it."

"Sure, D.D.A. Winters. Tell me what you need."

"About the guy who died last night—Charles Turner— he was in cell fifty-four in the tank before they took him to solitary, right?"

"I can check. Just a sec." There was a moment of silence, then, "Yeah. That's at the very end of the cell block."

"Alone?"

"It was crowded last night, but yeah, he's the only one listed."

If that were true, and Turner was alone in the cell, then that was proof he was moved for a reason other than overcrowding. Paul thought for a moment.

"What about the next cell?"

Jeff let out a laugh. "Oh, that's easy. It was Alfred."

"Alfred?"

"Alfred Washington." There was a pause, then, "You've never seen him around? He's a real character, sashays around in, uh, *flowery* apparel. You can't miss *her,* if you understand my meaning. Miss Washington wears a hairnet. I've tried to help Alfred, you know, get off the street, but so far no such luck. I think he's afraid of me because of my uniform."

At first Paul didn't understand, then he remembered. Despite David's emphasis on orgies of white and Negro men, the organization Jeff belonged to acted as a social network to help get work for members, housing for interracial couples—not an easy task—and undoubtedly aided those in trouble.

"They let him out yet?"

"This morning."

"What's his address?"

"No address. But I know where you can find him."

Paul put a dime on the counter and slipped a newspaper under his arm before returning to the car.

"I have a lead on someone who occupied the cell next to Charles Turner," he said as he shut the door.

Before he could continue, Blake started the car and looked over at him. His big hands gripped the wheel. "Where to?"

"No, it's better if I do this alone." Without thinking Paul reached over and touched Blake's sleeve. It was just a friendly gesture, but suddenly both of them felt awkward and couldn't seem to look at each other. Paul found his voice coming out gruff when he added, "I have a feeling this guy doesn't do well around cops."

Blake cleared his throat as he put the car in gear, and whatever discomfort had fallen between them seemed to dissipate. "Then I'll stay in the background," he replied firmly. "When we're done I'll bring you back here to your car."

"Fine." He gave the address where he wanted to go. "But there's something we need to do downtown after. It might take a few hours."

"I'm free all day. My next shift's Monday. What's up?"

"Sondergaard lied to us about what he was doing today."

"You mean lunch at the Cocoanut Grove?"

"I mean before. The time scheduled in his appointment book was between ten and noon. That's not a lunch. But look at this."

He unfolded the paper and showed him the headline:

COUNCIL VOTES TODAY
ON FUTURE OF BUNKER HILL
Disappearance of Councilman
Bullock may swing vote

"What do you think it means?" Blake asked, pulling into traffic.

"I don't know," Paul said somberly. "But whatever it is, it's bigger than we thought."

Chapter 5

As he crossed the park after being dropped off, Paul spotted someone he recognized getting off an electric streetcar that had slowed to a stop on Olive. It was Billy, the young man who had called David the night before and alerted them to Charles Turner's arrest. With a sinking feeling, Paul guessed what he was up to and promised to speak to the boy when he got a chance. Pershing Square had a reputation that Billy couldn't be unaware of. He was a smart kid, who hung out around the office on Hill Street several blocks north of here where David helped put out a homophile magazine in his free time. David had taken him under his wing as best he could, but his influence didn't stop Billy from using a series of fake I.D.s to get into places a sixteen-year-old had no business going. At least he was dressed in a manner that wouldn't bring attention to himself this morning, but Paul still didn't like it when he saw him sashaying his hips in a leisurely stroll through the park like he hadn't a care in the world.

The sky directly above was still a sharp blue from the winds the night before but there were already mustard-brown smudges on the horizon and the downtown air was thick with automobile exhaust. Over on Sixth Street he could see Blake's Hudson Hornet snarled in traffic as it circled the block. The park was filled with churchless preachers waving their bibles, Trotskyites shilling from soapboxes, shopgirls taking their morning break, and suited businessmen congregating with cups of steaming coffee. It didn't take long before he found the person he was looking for in a corner of the park.

"Are you Alfred Washington?"

Paul slipped onto a park bench already occupied by a rather gaunt young Negro who appeared on close inspection to be in his early twenties but at a glance might pass as an elderly woman. He was swathed as Jeff had described, in loose fitting flower-print apparel, though he had removed the net from his perfectly coiffed hair and replaced it with a bright red scarf tied like a turban. He was working knitting needles with slender, elegant hands with fingers that seemed to go on forever, and nails that were long for a man, but scrupulously clean; a colorful garment that appeared to be the beginnings of a scarf snaked its way from his lap down around his legs.

"It used to be beautiful here," Alfred said, as if in response to his question, "before they tore it all up. It was like a tropical island inhabited by queens, right in the center of the city."

Paul recalled what it had been like in Pershing Square before the urban renewal project had shorn the lush vegetation and replaced it with an underground garage to accommodate the ever increasing flow of automobiles into downtown, covered by a dismal park of flat lawn with sparse clusters of trees around its perimeter.

Of course, David had insisted somewhat heatedly that the project was a conspiracy of downtown businessmen to drive gays from the park, and looking around at the bleak surroundings, Paul couldn't entirely disagree.

The ornate turn-of-the-century three-tiered fountain at the center of the park, where men had congregated day and night to meet other men since the turn of the century, was gone, replaced by a modern pair, and what had been a jungle surrounding it had become a series of cement walkways cutting across a flat expanse of trimmed grass.

"There were overgrown little paths between the banana tree groves, bamboo thickets as high as a building." Alfred's eyes grew wide with the memory and he set down his needles. The flowing gesture of his long bony arms reminded Paul of the moves of a ballet dancer and he wondered if sometime in his past the young man had received dance training. "And at night, even with the lights of the Biltmore Hotel and all the other buildings, even with the moon and the stars, it was dark and wonderful in that tropical forest, and anything could happen."

"I remember," Paul said. He also remembered the periodic police sweeps, especially during election season, to drive such activities from the park. A Sisyphean task, if ever there was one, and even the decimation of its foliage couldn't kill Pershing Square's reputation, or stop men from coming here day and night, although they'd better have a room, because the days when you could get lost in the bushes were gone.

"My name's Paul Winters. I'm from the D.A.'s Office. I don't want you to be afraid. You're not in any trouble. I was just hoping you might be able to help me."

Alfred pursed his lips. "That pretty white boy lied when he said I came on to him."

"I'll do what I can to get those charges against you dropped. Will you help me if I help you?"

Out of the corner of his eye Paul noticed to his exasperation that Billy was parading himself back and forth on a path in front of several benches at the other end of the park. What was that kid up to? It was bad enough if he was trying to pick someone up, but then another idea crossed his mind which was much worse.

"You're handsome for a white boy," Alfred said, batting his eyelashes coyly as he started clicking up a storm with his knitting needles again.

Paul smiled at him, keeping Billy in the periphery of his vision, and forged on. "There was a man next to you in your cell last night. At the very end of the cell block. Do you remember him?"

"There were two."

"No, it was a man named Charles Turner. He was thin, in his thirties, well-dressed in a suit."

"Yes, I remember him. He recognized the other man."

Paul hesitated. He couldn't be sure how reliable Alfred's account might be, and yet, there was no one else to ask. "The other man?"

"The other man in his cell. They worked together. Or at least in the same place. The man you want to know about, he said to the other man that he recognized him from work."

"Tell me exactly what happened."

The clickety-click of the needles slowed, then stopped. "The other guy was brought in first. Then your friend. Then your friend was taken out to make his phone call, and a few minutes later they brought him back."

"And then what?"

"First they took the other guy out—"

"Who took him out?"

"Two cops."

"In uniform?"

"No, business suits."

Probably homicide detectives, Paul thought. He wondered if it was Falk and Vincent. "And then?"

"Later your friend was taken out, too. But it was another cop that did it. Plainclothed. One of the same ones who brought him in in the first place."

That would be Hollings or Ryan. But what had made him take Turner from his cell and bring him down to solitary? Not overcrowding. And what had become of the other man in the cell?

"Nothing happened other than that in the cell between the two men? No arguments, no fights? Nothing out of the ordinary?"

Alfred shook his head. That seemed to be the extent of his knowledge on the events the night before, so Paul thanked him, offered him a few dollars and promised to look into getting the charges against him dropped.

"The next time Officer Dupuis asks to help you—you know who he is, don't you? The colored policeman at the booking desk at Lincoln Heights Jail?—take him up on it. He's a good man, you can trust him."

As he set off across the park he grimly observed as Billy performed his little parade on the walkway. Damn that kid. If that boy was selling himself Paul was going to stop it right now even if he had to drag Billy by the nape of his neck out of the park. Then he realized the boy was trying to get the attention of a man dressed all in black who sat slouched against a park bench and utterly ignored him. There was no question the man was a hustler, no two ways about it. Paul laughed out loud and shook his head. If Billy was so naïve that he couldn't tell trade from a pick-up, he was probably safe as long as he didn't have any money in his pocket. He'd set the kid straight the next time he saw him, and there would be no more visits to Pershing Square.

Paul flagged down Blake, who'd just turned onto Fifth, and slid into the passenger seat.

"Do you know what Charles Turner did for a living?"

Blake hesitated a moment, then said, "He worked for the government. Accounting."

"What department?"

"Department of Transportation, why?"

"Someone he worked with in that department was in his cell. I think it was just a coincidence. Both men brought in the same night. I don't know why, but I think that's what got Charles Turner killed."

"Who was this other guy?"

"I don't know. There's no record of him being in that cell. And that probably means there's no record of his arrest. I think Falk and Vincent from Homicide are playing dirty. I'd like you to check Missing Persons. See if anybody has gone missing from the Department of Transportation accounting department."

"I can do that." Blake nodded.

"Maybe you can drop me off at City Hall for the council meeting. How about if we meet up once you check out Missing Persons?"

◇◇◇

The meeting was in full swing by the time Paul slid onto the long wooden church-pew-style benches in the city council chambers. He noticed Pritchard Sondergaard watching the proceedings, leaning in his white linen suit against a granite column in a side aisle, his fedora in his hand. When Paul looked back a moment later, the attorney was gone. The fourteen council members present were seated at the podium; one seat remained empty. An elderly professorial gentleman in spectacles was testifying by a standing microphone, leaning into it as if he were about to take a nibble.

"There is nothing wrong with the buildings in that neighborhood," he said. The microphone squealed, and he shrank back from it before continuing, while groans rose from the cringing packed audience. "They're old, yes, and

68

run down, but they are structurally sound and there's no reason to tear them all down."

"Except greed!" someone shouted from the audience.

Council President Armstrong, a jowly old goat of a man, frowned gravely from the podium and pounded a gavel. "We will clear these chambers if members of the public can't contain themselves. Is that understood?"

"Yes," the man sitting next to Paul muttered, "We can't have a little democracy in our city council hearings, can we?"

Paul looked over and found a stout little man with a stubby beard flecked with gray gazing at the funny papers as he listened to the hearing. The notepad and pen beside him as well as his world-weary air and rumpled clothes—and the fact that he was here at all—suggested to Paul that he was a reporter. His sleeves were rolled up and there were maritime tattoos on each forearm. Perhaps Paul still wouldn't have seen the connection if the man hadn't been smoking a pipe as well and reading Popeye the Sailor—but he did have a resemblance in appearance and grumbling temperament to the comic strip character.

The elderly man at the microphone went on, reading from a prepared statement in his hand, "The federal government has circled the neighborhood with a red line—like every neighborhood in America with more than a trace of minority population—which makes it difficult for homeowners and landlords to borrow money for mortgages or repairs…"

"Thank you Federal Housing Administration!" the reporter snickered. He noticed his pipe had gone out, pulled a pouch from his jacket, tamped down some tobacco, and lit up.

"…The inevitable result is dilapidated buildings. But this is a vibrant neighborhood with beautiful architecture that can be saved."

Bunker Hill was a neighborhood of late nineteenth century Victorian mansions that had deteriorated when their wealthy owners had seen greener pastures in Pasadena and in the new exclusive neighborhoods to the west. Over the years the beautiful homes had been split up into residential hotels and lodging houses for downtown hotel and shop employees and factory workers in the industrial area to the east. Most walked to work and few had cars.

"At least Mayor Bowron wasn't planning to throw nine thousand people out on the street," the reporter mumbled, puffing away on his pipe as the old man finished testifying and shuffled to his seat.

Fletcher Bowron had been the mayor of Los Angeles until an ugly red-baiting smear campaign orchestrated by the *Los Angeles Times*, in part over his plans for Bunker Hill, had driven him from office three years before. His administration's idea to raze the area and replace it with high rise apartments affordable to the present residents of the neighborhood had been replaced with a new plan more agreeable to the downtown business elite, who wanted to force the working class from their homes and replace them with an extended financial district, expensive housing and cultural centers like museums and theaters. A neighborhood for the future, a neighborhood friendly to the automobile—and less so to pedestrians and the people who worked to keep downtown running.

Paul had always considered Bowron a demagogue—he'd repeatedly made derogatory comments lamenting all the effeminate men and masculine women seen walking the streets of L.A.—but his administration's suggestions for Bunker Hill had been far more humane than the plan now being considered.

"Our time is up for scheduled testimony," Council President Armstrong announced. "It is now time for a vote on the matter."

An angry din rose among the public seated in the chambers.

A councilman on the far side of the podium leaned into his microphone. "This vote should be postponed until the return of Councilman Bullock! He has been an important spokesman for the residents of that neighborhood, a fierce defender of their rights. Why are we rushing this?"

Council President Armstrong raised an eyebrow. "Are you suggesting city business wait until he tires of his Tijuana love nest and comes back home?"

Laughter and guffaws carried from the crowd, but beneath it, murmurs of unrest.

"This isn't right," a councilwoman said. "We should wait until the entire council is here!"

"We cannot put off this vote indefinitely," the Council President countered. "The vote was scheduled for today, and it will be today."

"Yeah," the reporter grumbled. "No time left to discuss driving thousands from their homes and jobs." It took a moment for Paul to realize the reporter was addressing him now. He tipped his pipe at Paul, then flipped from the funny papers to the opinion page of his newspaper, and tapped at a column with his picture next to the byline. "Marvin Botwinick's the name," he said.

The *Los Angeles Daily* was a liberal paper, not large in circulation, but influential. It had campaigned rather brazenly against corruption in the city, and was disciplined enough to go after the very candidates it had endorsed when they strayed from the path.

Paul offered his hand. "I'm Paul Winters, a prosecutor with the D.A.'s office. You and I should have met a long time ago."

"I know who you are." Marvin grinned. "It's good to finally meet you. The question for me is, now that you're here, which of those lying bastards on the council are you planning to go after?"

"And who do you suggest I go after first?"

"Wait for the vote and you'll know." Between puffs of smoke, he commented, "Convenient that the swing vote and leading champion for the people of that neighborhood disappears days before the vote, and the sleaziest papers tied to big downtown business interests wage a smear campaign against him."

Paul remembered Jeannie's claim the night before regarding the sexual proclivities of Victoria Lynn, the actress Bullock was purported to have skipped town with. "What do you know about him running off with that actress?"

"Nothing. That's the problem. Everybody leaves a trail. Everybody. And there's absolutely no evidence he even left town. I couldn't validate one line of any of those sex scandal stories that have been heating up the tabloids."

After some finagling, the council began to take a vote. Two voted for the proposal, then two against. Another abstained, citing a conflict of interest, as he owned property on Bunker Hill. While another leaned forward toward his microphone on the podium and voted for the proposal, Paul glanced over to find Jim Blake slipping onto the bench on the other side of him.

"There was no listing for a missing person who worked at the Department of Transportation," Blake said quietly. "Are you sure they worked together?"

Again Paul wondered about the reliability of Alfred Washington's story. He shook his head grimly. "I can't be sure, but it's the only lead we have."

Three more councilmen voted for, three against.

"Look, there's another possibility," Blake said. "If our mystery guy disappeared last night, the Missing Person's

Bureau wouldn't take the report for twenty-four hours. That means perhaps as late as this evening."

"So what do we do?"

"We wait. We don't have any other choice. I'll keep on it."

The last two council members present voted, one for, one against. The plan had passed, seven to six, with one absence and one abstention. The audience rose to its feet, some applauding, others shouting angrily and waving their fists. The council members quickly disappeared into a door behind the podium.

Marvin Botwinick stood shaking his head. "Don't get me wrong. It's a shitty neighborhood. I wouldn't want to live there. But those people have got to live somewhere." He gathered up his note pad and folded his newspaper. "Actually, I'm kind of sweet on Bunker Hill. I rented a place there just after the war. I'd come from Brooklyn to set up a household for me and my bride. There weren't many neighborhoods that allowed Jews—at least ones we could afford after just getting out of the service—but when my wife arrived and saw the fourth floor walk-up I'd rented she marched right back to the train station and went back to Brooklyn."

"You're sweet on the neighborhood that made your wife leave you?"

He grinned. "Hey, she came back. I guess she must have loved me, huh? Got three kids now." He raised an eyebrow. "And we live in Culver City. Gotta go. Good to meet you." He handed Paul his card. "I have a column to put out by the evening edition. Headline: the bad guys just won again." He shuffled past them down the aisle, still puffing away, and disappeared into the crowd.

Blake looked at his wristwatch, and again Paul noticed the black hairs on the back of his large hand. "You free for lunch?"

Paul nodded, his eyes drifting beyond Blake's shoulder to a man in a white linen suit making his way through the crowd toward the podium.

"Yes," Paul said. "And I have just the place."

◇◇◇

Paul dialed his office to get his messages, then put in another dime and made a second call. He was watching Jim Blake through the glass door of the phone booth as the vice cop leaned against the opposite wall in the main entrance corridor of City Hall when a familiar voice came on the line.

"Look, David, something's come up. Is it okay if I cancel for lunch today?"

"I guess. What's wrong?"

"Nothing's wrong. I'm just a little behind at work."

A pause. "Oh, well, okay. There was something I wanted to tell you, but I guess it can wait. Where are you? I hear noise."

"Um, I'm actually in a phone booth at City Hall." Then, perhaps too quickly, "On a case."

There was a moment of silence over the line.

"So then, I'll see you tonight? Your place?"

"I'll see you tonight," Paul said.

◇◇◇

There was something that bothered Paul about the assemblage of several city council members sitting with Pritchard Sondergaard at a long table under a Moorish arch at the Cocoanut Grove, but he couldn't put his finger on it. He noted that his boss the District Attorney was not in attendance despite the claim earlier in the morning by the white-linen-suited lawyer that he would be, and Paul chalked it up to the legendary one-upmanship Sondergaard relished in and out of the courtroom.

He and Blake were seated far across the room from them, with an empty dance floor and tables filled with snappily dressed couples between. Lushly fronded palm trees with hanging stuffed monkeys—rumored to have come from Rudolph Valentino's *The Sheik*—also served to shield them from view. Paul wasn't ready to confront Sondergaard directly again, or to provoke him, but he wanted to see exactly who the players were in the unfolding drama he didn't yet understand.

"That's the power in the city, right there," Paul said. "They've got the biggest papers behind them, the business lobby, everything it takes to get things done and to convince the public it's in their best interests."

"And what's that got to do with Charles Turner's death?"

Paul shook his head and smiled, crushing his cigarette in an ashtray. "I have no idea. No idea at all." He glanced over the menu, noticed the steaks were over five dollars, and wondered if he should offer to pay, considering what an LAPD cop's salary amounted to. He could always tell Blake that he'd put it on his expense account, even though he didn't have one.

Blake took in the spacious surroundings, nodding, clearly impressed. "Ever been here before?"

"Just once." It had been a magical night, just six months ago, the third time he had been out with David, to celebrate his graduation from creative arts school, and Paul had wanted to impress him. After the floorshow, with its scantily clad dancers, Sammy Davis Jr. had performed. Later David couldn't stop talking about it: the midnight blue ceiling glittering with stars, the magnificent staircase that led down to the restaurant, the dance floor packed with glamorous couples, Judy Garland with her entourage at a table nearby, the women in their sequined gowns, the men so handsome in their spiffy suits. Paul had gazed into David's eyes all night long, wanting only to hold him, to take him out on the dance floor. He had settled for sliding his leg under the table and letting it press against David's.

A bow-tied waiter came up to take their order.

"I'll have the sirloin, rare, and a glass of red wine." Paul handed him the menu.

"Same for me," Blake said. As the vice cop gave the waiter his menu, Paul noticed the furrow in his brow that he'd seen the night before was a permanent fixture, a hard line rising from his left eyebrow, an angry twin to the cleft in his chin. He also became aware again what a big man he was, shoulders so wide Paul couldn't see the back of his chair behind him. Tall and slender and weighing in at one-seventy, Paul figured Blake must have at least fifty pounds on him, maybe more.

"You live here all your life?" Blake took out a new pack of Chesterfields and broke the cellophane.

Paul grinned. "That obvious? You can tell I have orange groves in my blood? Yeah, I'm L.A. born and bred. Culver City, actually. Went to UCLA, and after that, directly into the D.A.'s Office. You said you came from Wisconsin. What brought you out here?"

Blake lit up, tossed the match in the tray. "I'd had shore leave here during the war. I guess it pulled me back."

"The sand and the sun, summer all year long?"

"Something like that."

"You don't look old enough to have been in the war. What are you—thirty?"

Blake nodded. "Almost. I did a little lying to get in. There wasn't much for me back home."

"A lot of people ended up here after the war. Here, San Francisco, New York. They just couldn't go home afterwards. I guess the war changed them." He paused, then went on, eyeing Blake closely. "Or they learned things about themselves they didn't know before."

If Paul had offered bait, Blake didn't bite. Exhaling through his nostrils, he waved the plume of smoke away. "I thought about staying. But things happened, and in the end, I went back. Ten years."

Paul observed him for a moment. "This morning you said you had known someone who had committed suicide before."

Blake's lip became a fine line and for a time he didn't speak. In the soft light of the dining room, his eyes had taken on that startling blue with fissures of black, and once again Paul was taken aback by how striking they were. "A navy buddy of mine."

"During the war?"

"Just after. During demobilization. Just before everybody was discharged to go home." There was a bitter twist to his mouth, as if his cigarette hadn't tasted the way he thought it would. "Here. Here in L.A."

The waiter brought their plates and made a show of pouring each a glass of wine. Before he took a bite, Blake shook a heavy dose of salt over his meal. They dug into their steaks with knives and forks and didn't talk for a while.

Paul took a sip of wine and glanced at Blake casually. "Are you married?"

"Naw," Blake said. He paused, picked up his cigarette, took a drag, poked at the ash tray with it, then added, "I mean, I'd like to be, if the right girl came along. I was seeing someone back in Wisconsin, a really nice girl, for a long time, but it didn't work out." He went back to attacking his steak. "When I left Milwaukee I guess that ended it for good. There was something not quite right between us, you know?" He cocked his head thoughtfully. "I probably should have broken up with her sooner. In the end, I think, I probably treated her pretty badly. I guess I just didn't feel the same about her as she felt about me." He didn't look up, concentrating on his steak, stabbing what was left with his fork and slicing it into bite sized pieces with the knife. "How about you? I don't see a ring on your finger. A nice looking guy like you, you aren't married?"

"Me?" Paul swallowed and picked up his wine glass quickly. "No. I guess you could say I'm married to my job, you know, it's hard to fit it all in, a career... and the rest. I suppose you could say I'm a confirmed bachelor."

Blake pushed back his plate and lit another cigarette, watching him a moment. "I can understand that. I read up a little on you." He exhaled smoke and grinned. "You're famous. In the papers."

"Oh, I don't know about that." Paul felt heat come to his cheeks and groped for his cigarette pack in his pocket.

Blake nodded, still watching him. "No, really. I admire that. A guy who builds a successful career, that's something I think very highly of."

Paul lit up and checked his watch. "I've got to get back to the office soon." He tilted his head and gazed across the room at the men assembled at the long table under the Moorish arch, and a little smile came to his face. "I just figured out what it was that was bothering me," he said, nodding to himself as he continued to observe them. "Look at them. Do you see what they all have in common?"

Blake set down his glass and leaned back to see around the trunk of a nearby palm tree. He stared at the seven council members for a long while. "What?"

"Each and every one voted to sell out Bunker Hill."

78

Chapter 6

That evening when Dr. Stone arrived home he was tired and irritable. His introduction to detectives from various divisions that afternoon had not gone as he would have hoped, and it would be an understatement to say some had been bluntly skeptical regarding his suggestions on improving interrogation techniques. He understood he had to be patient. He was, after all, elbowing into their turf, and a little resentment was to be expected. Members of law enforcement were not known for their flexibility or lack of ego, and he couldn't expect new ideas from an as-yet-unproven source to be accepted without a fight. He needed to wait for a case to come along to make a name for himself. It would happen.

Susan met him at the front door in her apron with his nightly martini, as she always did, accompanied by good smells of dinner cooking in the kitchen. He wished that the female of the species could understand that from as far back as the days of the cave man, males needed a little space when they came home, to unwind, to read the mail, to relax, and the smothering effects of an attentive chattering woman was the last thing they wanted. But, of course, he knew she was only trying to please him.

"Your mother called long distance again," she began, giving him a quick peck on the cheek and handing him the martini glass. "I don't know why she calls during the day when she knows you aren't home until six."

"She knows you'll listen to her prattle no matter how long she goes on." He took a sip and calculated that his drink had been mixed perfectly, a relief since that wasn't always the case.

"She must be spending a fortune." She smiled warmly. "Michael spoke to her on the phone today. It was so cute."

"I'm sure she loved that."

He placed his free hand on her swelling abdomen. "How's my baby?"

"Impatient. I felt a kick this afternoon."

Michael called from the dining room, "Daddy, come quick!"

"He built a house today," Susan explained, heading for the kitchen. She paused at the door, adding, "Tonight we're having your favorite!" and disappeared inside.

He had politely complimented her first attempt at roast beef when they were newlyweds. One time. In her mind ever since it was his favorite meal and he found himself sentenced to a lifetime of roast beef every Friday night. He went through the living room and found Michael sitting between two chairs from the dining table draped with a rose colored blanket to create a roof over his head.

"How's my little man?"

"Daddy!"

"Do you have a little house?"

Michael nodded enthusiastically.

"Let's see if we can make it a little bit better." He set his martini glass aside and went to the linen closet and found a blue blanket and pulled it from the shelf. Michael stared at him with big puzzled eyes as he replaced the rose blanket with the blue.

"How's that, little man?" He waited for Michael to nod, uncomprehendingly, then said, "Now, your daddy is going to wash up, and then Mommy is going to serve us dinner."

Stone went into the bathroom and washed his hands. When he reached for a towel, he stiffened in dismay. "Susan, could you come here a moment?" he called.

She appeared in the bathroom doorway with a spatula in her hand, a quizzical expression on her face.

"I have asked one thing of you, and only one thing. To rotate these towels daily. Is that asking too much?"

He had explained to her, rather patiently, that by rotating the towels for the sink with the ones by the bathtub, he'd always have a dry towel to use. But it never seemed to sink in, in four years of telling her, and it was difficult to keep a clipped tone from his voice.

She turned her head away from him.

"Are you going to cry? If you are, I'm going to be very angry with you."

She stood frozen in place, her face angled away from him.

"When I ask a question, I don't think it's expecting too much to get an answer."

She made a move to go, and he caught her wrist.

"Is it expecting too much?"

She shook her head, still facing away.

"Is expecting a verbal answer from my wife too much?"

"No." Her voice quavered.

"Of course it isn't." He brought her to him and hugged her tightly. She resisted at first, the sullen side of her personality coming through that he found so tiresome, but he knew how to take care of that.

"You look beautiful tonight." He tapped her nose and smiled. He could feel her soften, as she always did, butter melting into him. "You're glowing." He caressed her cheek. "I don't think you've ever been more lovely." Of course it wasn't true. She looked positively bovine. She always gained too much weight when she was pregnant, weight she wouldn't be able to lose once the baby was born. His mother had warned him that this was the fate of big-boned women who liked to cook, but of course he hadn't listened.

"Did I thank you for cooking my favorite tonight?" he asked.

She wiped her cheeks and put on a smile. "I know how much you like it."

"Now go ahead, I'll be right with you." He patted her playfully on the fanny as she turned to go.

Grimacing, he went to the rack by the tub and got a dry towel.

It was a cop bar like any other cop bar, and in the end, they were all the same. This one had rich mahogany paneling and a big mirror above the bar, with tables and booths bathed in shadows. Detective Ryan was sitting alone on a stool at the bar, nursing a scotch and staring fixedly at wet rings made from the glass when Blake slid onto the stool next to him. The place was almost empty, but it was early. After every shift the establishment was packed, but it wouldn't get much noisier than it was now.

The bartender nodded at him and he ordered a Budweiser. Ryan acknowledged his presence by patting him on the shoulder with drunken affection.

"You're a good kid, you know?" Ryan said. "And I have a little piece of advice for you. You ought to get on a train and go back to wherever you came from. And you want to know why? Because nobody respects cops in this city, nobody. And when they treat you like dirt, it makes you dirty."

Blake wondered if Ryan might be referring to himself; he figured the detective's kick-back scheme with Pritchard

Sondergaard probably wasn't the only way he made an extra buck.

The bartender brought his beer and gave Blake a knowing glance while he pierced the can with an opener. "Need a glass?" Blake shook his head and the barman retreated to the other end of the bar.

Blake took a swig, glanced around to make sure none of the few other patrons were within hearing distance, and said, "I need you to tell me something. About the guy last night. Charles Turner, the guy I arrested. What happened when you brought him up to his cell?"

Ryan cocked his head and observed him with an assessing, almost sober gaze. "Now why would you be asking me that?"

"Because he's dead and I want to know why."

Shaking his head and shrugging, Ryan said, "The queers do that every day. Kill themselves. Can you blame them? Who knows, maybe the poor bastard's better off now."

"I want to know why he ended up in solitary rather than in the Fruit Tank."

Ryan blinked, his eyes shiny black orbs. "We did bring him to the tank." His thick brows grew together, his tone defensive. "At first."

"What happened?"

He signaled for the bartender to refill his glass before he answered. When the bartender had faded back into the shadows again, and Ryan had taken a slow sip, he said, "We left him there. We took him up with that guard."

"Was the tank overcrowded?"

"No. I mean, it was a busy night. There'd been raids over on La Brea. But there was just one other guy in Turner's cell."

That confirmed what the colored inmate in the next cell had told Paul Winters this morning in Pershing Square. "Okay, how did he turn up dead in the solitary cell block?"

"The phones were busy when we booked him, you remember? So a few minutes later Hollings and I take him down for his phone call and for the nigger at the booking desk to take his belongings. We bring him back to his cell, and we think that's it. But downstairs, Lieutenant Falk from homicide gets this call, I don't know who it was from, balling him out. I could hear the guy yelling at him and I was all the way down the hall. Then he and his partner, you know, what's his name, Vincent, bring down the guy who was Turner's cell mate and usher him out of the jail."

"You have any idea where they went?"

Shaking his head, Ryan took another drink. "None whatsoever. Could have been letting him go for all I know."

"I still don't see how this gets Turner in solitary."

"Before they left, Falk tells us to take him down to the solitary block." He shrugged uneasily, the hand that wasn't holding his drink resting on his beer belly. "We just did what we were told."

"And now a man's dead."

"I told you this was a dirty town."

"So you and Hollings brought him down—"

"No, I did it alone," Ryan interrupted. "I left the queer in his cell in solitary and I don't know what happened to him after that."

"And Hollings?"

Ryan stared into his drink, mesmerized by the dark liquid. "Hollings didn't like it. He said the whole thing stank. Just the way they dragged that guy out of there, not stopping off at the booking desk, nothing. It just didn't seem right."

Blake closed his eyes for a second in dismay, then opened them. "Hollings followed them."

Ryan nodded. He was rambling now, too far gone, in his own world. "He's a good man, a good cop. And what does it get you? They tried to make him dirty, but they couldn't." He slouched against the bar as if he could hardly stay balanced on the stool, and muttered like he was reciting a litany, "You should get on a train and go back to where you came from."

Blake wasn't going to get anything more out of him. Setting his empty beer can on the bar, he pushed back his stool. "Where is he now? I want to talk to him."

"He's gone." Ryan seemed to have disappeared into his glass. "I haven't seen him since last night when he tailed Falk and Vincent. He just vanished without a trace. Never went home to his wife last night. Didn't show up for work today. Just gone." He finally looked up at Blake, bleary eyed, and snapped his finger. "Like *that*."

Dinner had not gone exactly as planned, and after showering Paul stood naked in the bathroom brushing his teeth ferociously in front of the mirror, while David brooded in the living room reading a book with the local news blaring on the television. He had forgotten when he'd cancelled lunch this afternoon that David had said there was something he wanted to talk about. Over a candlelit dinner of wine and spaghetti in the kitchen nook David had reminded him of the job application he had sent along with his portfolio to a New York ad agency. He had spoken to them over the phone a few weeks ago, and then nothing, until today. They had offered to fly him in for an interview next week.

"If I go, you know," he'd said softly, toying pensively with the stem of his wine glass, "they're going to hire me. They wouldn't be paying for my air fare and hotel if they weren't serious. It would mean moving to New York."

"They're offering you a free vacation in New York City, take it. We can deal with all the other stuff if you get the job."

David looked hurt and grimaced. "Some vacation. I'd be by myself."

Paul felt like a total cad saying, "We always knew you were too good for L.A. New York is the place you've got to be if you want a great advertising career. And they're wasting you in that job you have now." David was working in a small agency on Wilshire with a mostly conservative local clientele, hardly a fit for the cutting-edge ideas and quirky humor that had attracted New York to his talent. "I don't want you to go, but I don't think it's fair for me to hold you back."

"Oh," David said. "This is you being noble."

"You know how much I care about you, and you know how much fun we have together..."

"Do you realize how patronizing that is?"

Paul had thrown up his hands, exasperated. "What do you want from me? You ask me what I think, then when I tell you, you get mad at me." He sighed, shaking his head. "Sometimes, you and I, we're just on different wavelengths, that's all."

The soft candlelight flickering in David's face couldn't hide that his mouth had become a hard line. "How so?"

"Well, you know, it just so happens some of the stuff you're involved in makes me uncomfortable and could get me in a lot of trouble. One slip, and it would be over for me at the D.A.'s Office, you know that."

"Now we're talking about *your* career."

"Yes, *my* career, one I have worked very hard to be successful at, one I don't want to be destroyed because you have all these dreams and ideas that won't come true for a hundred years."

"They won't come true if no one stands up and tries to change things."

"You realize that organization you belonged to last year was founded by communists, don't you?"

"Oh my God, you are seriously going to red-bait me over wine and spaghetti?"

"David, it's not funny. People are losing their jobs and their careers because they signed a petition twenty years ago when they were college freshmen."

David put down his fork and folded his arms across his chest. "So you sit back and do nothing."

"You don't seem to understand what a dangerous world it is out there for people like us, and it makes me afraid for you. I've seen what happens to people who make the kind of mistakes you seem willing—for both of us—to make."

"And what is the price of doing nothing?"

"You have a job you don't like that doesn't challenge you. You have nothing to lose!"

"Thank you."

Paul sighed. "I'm sorry." He dropped his napkin on the table and pushed back his plate. "How come every conversation we have about you and me ends up being about politics?"

They'd cleaned up and washed and dried the dishes bantering neutrally about mutual friends and this weekend's weather forecast; there hadn't been much to say after that as the evening passed.

Now Paul went after his molars with his brush with the intensity of a housewife with a Brillo pad attacking a stain in a TV commercial. While everything Paul said regarding David's job interview was true, he knew it wasn't what David wanted to hear, and now he felt angry with himself for being so cruel and angry with David for needing him so much and for knowing exactly what he wanted and for making him feel so guilty for giving him good advice.

And he had to ask himself, why was he wrecking his relationship with a really good guy, one who really cared for him? He was so good at planning out each step of his career, understanding how one stone provided the foundation for the next, why couldn't he do that with his relationships? Why was he so damn restless? Why couldn't he just be happy with what he had?

Well, at least, he thought brutally, if David moved to New York it would end all those little hints about moving in together, something that was absolutely impossible under any circumstances. Living with another guy in his apartment would do wonders for his career.

Over the water running in the sink, he thought he heard a snippet about the city council vote this afternoon on the local news, and scurried into the living room to hear what it was. By the time he got there whatever the newsman had mentioned regarding Bunker Hill was over and a commercial was playing. He turned the volume knob down.

David was lounging on the couch eating a bowl of cereal. He had a mystery novel by Edgar Box open on the table beside him. He had explained to Paul the name was a pseudonym for the writer Gore Vidal, who, after writing an acclaimed bestseller about his experiences in World War II had written a novel which created a furor because of its frank portrayal of homosexual culture. The outraged *New York Times* book review set out to destroy the young author's career, refusing to review or accept advertising for his future books; Vidal had been forced to write under a pseudonym to survive.

When David looked at him inquisitively, Paul turned all his anger and confusion on him. He realized he looked rather foolish standing there naked with a toothbrush in his hand. "Must you eat in here?" he demanded. "Everywhere

I go there's a trail of cereal on the carpet. That's what they made dining room tables for."

"Who knew?" David munched on another mouthful with the look of an innocent on his face. He seemed to have gotten over their earlier argument and the amused curve of his lip told Paul he was in a playful mood. "You never complained before."

"Yes, but I'm getting a little tired of always cleaning up after you. I can't even get into bed without finding Wheaties between the sheets."

"I guess it's like you walking around the house brushing your teeth."

"No, it's not the same because I don't leave a trail of toothpaste wherever I go."

"What about there?" David pointed at Paul's feet, fighting the grin that was spreading across his face. "You just dripped. I saw it. You don't realize that I go around with a paper towel wiping up your messes all the time. If I didn't there'd be Pepsodent stains all over the carpet."

Paul looked down and of course there was a drop of frothy toothpaste in the nap, the very first time ever, he was sure, that this had happened.

"Don't worry," David said magnanimously. "I'll clean it up." And then, under a theatrical sigh as he chomped down the last spoonful of his cereal, "I always do." He set the bowl aside and said, "Come over here."

Paul took a few grudging steps forward and David reached out and held on to his penis, stroking it.

"Feeling better?"

"A little," he said through toothpaste lathered in his mouth as he felt himself engorging.

The telephone rang—two quick buzzes, a pause, two quick buzzes—which meant it was for him, not the party that shared the line. Paul looked over his shoulder at the phone then at David. He made a move to answer it, but David was having none of it.

"Are you going to let me go?"

"Under the circumstances," David said, acknowledging the hardening rod, "I don't think that's bloody likely, do you?"

Paul sighed with gentle exasperation and pulled away from him, David's hand releasing him reluctantly. He padded into the kitchen, spit out the toothpaste, tossed the brush in the sink and went for the phone on the table by the front door, his erection bouncing as he went.

He was surprised to find Jim Blake on the other end. He felt that adrenaline rush in his chest that he experienced every time he'd been with the vice cop, and there was something intimate in just having his resonant voice so close to his ear. He glanced at David guiltily, but he had already gone back to reading his book.

"Sorry to reach you at home, but there've been a few developments."

"No problem, no problem at all. What's up?"

Blake told him about his conversation with Ryan, and while it fit in with what Paul had suspected, it didn't answer bigger questions he had, and the part about Sergeant Hollings disappearing made no sense at all. Again he had the feeling that the death of Charles Turner was a cog on a very large wheel and would shed little light on the bigger picture.

"Oh," Blake continued, "I have something else. The other guy in the cell, I have a name. Peter O'Keife. His wife called him in missing today. She actually called Missing Persons yesterday when he didn't come home for dinner, but they wouldn't take the report for twenty-four hours."

"Works for the Department of Transportation?"

"Yeah. I called over there and talked to a supervisor who hadn't left for the day yet. The two never worked together, not even on the same floor. Maybe they saw one another in the elevator, knew each other by sight."

A wrinkle appeared between Paul's eyebrows. "So there was no direct connection."

"The fact that Charles Turner recognized him at all seems to be enough to have gotten him killed."

Paul knew why Charles Turner was in that cell, but what about Peter O'Keife? What was his alleged crime?

"Any record of an arrest?"

"Nothing. O'Keife was totally clean."

To Paul that meant a worst-case scenario, where LAPD officers, most likely Lieutenant Falk and Detective Vincent, had taken a man off the street for unknown reasons and thrown him in a jail cell with no accountability. It stank of a conspiracy and a cover-up, and yet he had absolutely no clue as to what it was about. He didn't even want to think about where Peter O'Keife might be now.

"Let's see if we can find out exactly what O'Keife was doing at the Department of Transportation. Whatever it was, it was powerful enough to get Turner killed just by association."

"I have the wife's address. They live in the Valley."

"Can we meet, say ten tomorrow morning, and go talk to her?"

"Sure. Should I pick you up at your place?"

Paul turned his head and gazed at David on the couch, still enwrapped in his book. "Uh, no, I think it would be better if we met at the District Attorney's Office."

He had a sense that Blake wanted to add something else, and he hesitated before saying goodbye. "Anything more?"

He heard Blake swallow and take a breath before he answered.

91

"I wasn't honest with you before. I told you that Charles Turner had touched me and that was why I arrested him, but it wasn't true. Not really. I mean, he touched me, but not in that way. I just panicked. I got spotted as a vice cop and I just grabbed him so I could make an arrest. He's dead because of me."

There was a long moment of silence over the line.

"I wasn't sure if I could trust you when we met," Paul admitted slowly. "Even today, I had my doubts." He paused for a long moment, then said, "I trust you now."

When he hung up the phone, he stared at it for a moment, then he looked down and realized he had been stroking his cock all along and it was hard as a rock.

Jim Blake sat down on the bed in his rented room and picked up a bottle of rye from the lamp table and poured generously into a spotty glass he hadn't rinsed out from the night before. He took a gulp and felt the sting in his throat, and then the warmth spread throughout his stomach.

How many nights had he played out this scenario in different rooms in different towns? And in the end it always brought him back to a sticky summer day in L.A. with a pale yellow sky when armed military guards came into the barracks and took Jack Spencer away. He still remembered those hours of lying to himself, the pacing, then playing cards with the guys, guys who had always been friends but somehow couldn't quite look at him now, insisting in his mind that everything would be okay, ticking off all the other reasons Jack could have been taken into custody.

And all the while that terrible roiling feeling in his stomach, far worse than the tense sick exhilaration of battle, an anxiety he couldn't remember ever experiencing before, an ache that never seemed to quite leave him since.

Then, in the late hours of the night, they came for him, too. The crushing shame he felt, like pinpricks that made his face burn, made him want to peel his skin off like a mask and become someone else. The interrogation lasted until the early morning hours, his fervent, unequivocal denials, his angry denunciation of everything Jack had told them, and the growing realization that they believed him and the soaring relief that brought, that he was in the clear, that nobody would believe otherwise.

Blake stripped down to his boxers and poured himself another drink. He stared into the glass, lost for a moment in the amber liquid. Then he slipped into the bed and turned off the lamp. Sitting up, propped against pillows, the glass cradled in both hands, resting above his belly button on the soft line of hair that ran from a patch at his navel to his chest, he gazed into the soothing dimness of the room. The drawn curtains glowed from streetlights on Franklin and the gentle hiss of traffic was the only sound.

He took another drink, felt that warmth, sighed, drunk now, no doubt about it, and thought about the last time he had seen Jack Spencer alive, maybe the bitterest memory of all. The things Jack had said to him, things he didn't want to hear. And what he had said back. He recalled the hard cold edge of his voice more than the words themselves, perhaps realizing for the first time that tone could do more to lacerate than anything he could have said.

On Franklin a car backfired and a jolt ran through him ragged as electric current. His whole body tensed as it had that night upon hearing the shot and knowing with terrible finality what it meant, that everything he feared and everything he wanted was gone in an instant.

Blake drained his glass, groped for the bottle in the darkness, held it unsteadily as its neck clinked on the rim of the glass, and poured what was left from the bottle.

He took a sip then set his glass on the table for later, hoping it would be enough to get him through the night.

Chapter 7

They took the Hollywood freeway, which had recently been expanded from a half-mile stretch downtown and now extended all the way into the Valley. The median between lanes going opposite directions was empty now, the Red Cars gone, the tracks torn up. At least it might provide space for extra lanes, for the thoroughfare was experiencing twice its original projected capacity, and rush hour traffic had become a miserable parking lot for commuters from the Valley into downtown. But that would all change, the public was assured, once all the other proposed super highways were completed and snaked their way throughout the city.

"I've never been out here before," Blake said, taking a drag off his Chesterfield. Outside the open window, scruffy hills with red-tiled roofs hid the art deco band shell of the Hollywood Bowl on the left and a few moments later the flat bowl of the Valley spread out before them, a bright morning haze resting on the blue hills at the horizon.

"There was never much to see," Paul replied, "except oranges."

Tract homes were going up everywhere now, eating away at the groves that had once dominated the area. Organized urban planning had been tossed out the window in favor of providing homes for middle class post-World War II families quickly, and the haphazard growth had forgotten parks and open spaces originally envisioned by city designers. And yet, this was the dream municipal leaders had promised. An affordable home with a yard on clean streets a quick jaunt away from the bustle of the city.

They passed unfinished frame houses made of lath and tar paper and chicken wire—looking like shanties until workmen wielding trowels sloppy with stucco transformed them into cozy starter homes for growing families—and Paul wondered, as he always did seeing the way buildings were constructed in Southern California, how any of them could ever hope to stand in a wind storm. And yet they did, decade after decade.

Blake turned up a recently paved street of new homes, modest ramblers bright with fresh coats of paint. The sidewalks had yet to be put in, though wooden forms had been set up where the concrete was to be poured. A group of a dozen kids on bikes congregated at the corner, playing cards clipped in the spokes.

The Hudson Hornet slowed to a stop in front of a blue house with yellow shutters; fledgling bushes sprouted in a yard of newly planted velvet-green grass. As they got out of the car, a woman spotted them in the front window of the house and came out onto the porch. She had dirty blonde wavy hair that almost reached her shoulders and a pretty freckled face strained with worry. She must have been in her mid-thirties. She pulled off her apron and smoothed out her pink with white polka-dots dress as she descended the stairs and started down the cement walk toward them.

"I'm Paul Winters with the Los Angeles District Attorney's Office; this is Officer Blake. Did you report your husband, Peter O'Keife, missing last night?" He could see the pain in her eyes and felt sympathy for her immediately.

"Yes, thank you for coming. I'm Mrs. O'Keife. Have you heard anything?"

"I'm afraid not." Paul threw Blake a glance, hit with a wave of guilt for not telling her what little they knew. But until he was sure what had happened to her husband, offering confusing bits of information even he didn't understand seemed unnecessarily cruel. "We're here to find out as much as we can, Mrs. O'Keife. The more we know, the more likely we'll be able to find your husband."

A warm breeze was blowing down the street, rattling the leaves in young trees planted in young yards, but she put her hand to her throat as if she was suddenly cold.

"Children!" she called. "I want you to play in the back yard. Come on, hear?"

Paul noticed that three of the kids down the block had hair like hers.

"Aw, Mom!" the eldest blond, about eleven, protested. "We're having fun."

"Do as I say now, and if you're good we'll go for ice cream after lunch."

That seemed to placate them and the three blonds in the group untangled themselves from the rest of the neighborhood kids and made their way up the street in a parade of shiny bicycles and hair gleaming in the morning sunshine to the flagstone path leading around the side of the house. Once they disappeared and the fence latch clicked shut she seemed more relaxed.

"Please," she said, managing a brief polite smile. "If you'll come inside."

They followed her up the porch stairs and she opened the screen door for them. The living room was furnished in Early American, with framed stitched samplers offering sentimental homilies on the walls, a recliner that was obviously the "dad's chair" in a corner, and a floral-print couch facing a matching love seat in front of the fireplace, whose mantel held an array of brass framed family pictures. It was a homey setup, Paul thought, with nothing out of place except a broken pastel McCoy vase that lay in pieces on the dining table, a bent lampshade and a square of plywood over the window in the kitchen back door. The price of three active kids, he supposed. And then, when he remembered the look in her eyes, another darker notion occurred to him.

"Please," Mrs. O'Keife said. "Can I offer you some tea? I just set the kettle on the stove."

"That would be nice," Blake said. Paul said yes too because he knew the ritual of preparing tea would calm her.

"If you'll go ahead and have a seat I'll be right with you." She smoothed her dress again, as if she saw wrinkles that weren't there, and went into the kitchen. Paul could see her putting cups on a tray as he sat on the couch next to Blake. For a moment she leaned against the counter as if summoning the strength to go on, then steeled herself and took the kettle from the burner as it began to shriek. Outside the dining room window, he could hear the children shouting in their games.

When she came out with the tray of steaming cups and set it on the coffee table, Mrs. O'Keife took a cup for herself and sat on the love seat across from them.

"Mind if I smoke?" Blake asked, pulling a pack from his suit jacket.

"No, of course not," she said, indicating an ash tray on the table. He offered her one, and she took it. He lit them both off one match.

"I haven't had one of these in years," she reflected softly. "Since the war. Peter doesn't like it. I stopped for him when we were married."

"We have the report," Paul began, taking a cup and dropping a cube of sugar in. "But we'd like you to go over it with us from the beginning. Was there any indication that something was wrong? Was he acting normally before his disappearance?"

"He started acting strangely about a week and a half ago." Again her eyes, brown and thickly lashed, flickered with pain and worry. "He came home very late from work, upset. He didn't want to talk about it. He wasn't sure but he thought something was wrong and he didn't know who to go to for help."

"He works for the Department of Transportation, right? What does he do?"

"Peter is an accountant. His department allocates the money from the federal government and the state to build the freeways. There have been overruns, I'm sure you've heard, and a lot of the freeways they've been planning may never be built."

"You think he was worried about that?"

"No, this was something different. He wasn't sure, but he said he had to check the numbers again. A few days later—that would be Friday evening last week—he came home with a stack of papers. Six inches thick. He wanted to go over them over the weekend. I got a sense he had taken them without his boss knowing and he'd get into trouble if anyone found out. He spent both days hovering over them at the dining room table until his eyes were bleary."

"Did you look at them?" Blake asked. He shot a plume of smoke to the ceiling.

"He didn't want me to."

"But you did," he persisted gently.

She nodded silently, tapping a bullet of ash in the tray. "He took a bath Saturday night. I saw him hide the papers in the closet first. I couldn't help myself. But I couldn't make head or tail of them."

"What were they?"

"It was just numbers, mostly numbers."

"Like a budget?"

"I guess so... reports... financial stuff... it didn't mean anything to me. I got a sense that it wasn't all Department of Transportation documents, that Peter was following a trail, that one thing was leading to another. It was all held together with a big red rubber band."

The back door in the kitchen flew open and a girl of about eight with a blonde curly mop came bawling into the living room. She had freckles on her face just like her mother. "Mom, I cut my hand!" She held out a blood-tipped finger.

Mrs. O'Keife rose, setting her tea cup on the table. "Let's go get that washed off, honey."

The blond boy appeared in the kitchen doorway. "I can do it." He glanced at Paul and Blake curiously then took his little sister by the hand and led her to the bathroom. "It's my fault. She had her finger in the spokes when I spun my bike wheel."

"Thank you, Mitchell," she said, watching them go. "The Band-Aids are in the cabinet." Once they were gone, tears came to her eyes and she quickly crossed the carpet and stared out the dining room window, her arms tightly wrapped around her, the cigarette wedged between her fingers, a wisp of smoke rising.

Paul got up and went to her. "I'm sorry, Mrs. O'Keife, I know how upsetting this must be for you."

She didn't answer at first, just gazed beyond the low back fence into the scores of tract houses under construction beyond. "I worked just northeast of here during the war," she said tonelessly, almost to herself. "At an aerospace plant making parts for the military. It was mostly orange groves here then. They seemed to go on forever. It seemed far from the city back then."

"Who did you work for?"

"Rocketdyne. It was mostly women because all the boys were off in the Pacific or in Europe." She paused, taking a drag off her cigarette, then said, "After the war they didn't want us to work anymore. The men had come home."

Her whole body began to quiver and Paul placed his hand gently on her shoulder. Her face began to melt into tears. "Something's happened to him," she said. "I know it. It's not like him. He loves his family so much. He would never just disappear without letting anybody know where he was going."

"The missing persons report you filed last night said he didn't come home on Thursday night, is that right?"

She nodded anxiously, wiping her tears. "I don't want to look like this in front of the kids." She put on a weak apologetic smile. "Let's sit down." They returned to the living room and took their seats. She crushed her cigarette in the ash tray, and seemed to have regained her composure, answering his question, "He went to work Thursday morning and he never came home."

"We've spoken with his supervisor. He was at work on Thursday like always and he left at his regular time. If something happened to your husband, it happened after work."

Blake leaned forward on the couch. "Mrs. O'Keife, the papers he had taken from work, what happened to them? Did he bring them back to work?"

"I don't know. I think he was afraid the people at work might be the problem. He didn't know who to trust in the department." She refilled their cups with steaming tea and it occurred to Paul that in her mind no amount of turmoil was an excuse to keep her from being a proper hostess. "He met with a city councilman on Monday morning, I know that. He had taken the papers with him when he went. That night he didn't have the papers when he came home. He told me that we didn't have to worry about it anymore, that everything was going to be okay, and we shouldn't talk about it anymore. I think he seemed relieved after that. Everything went back to normal, except for the break-in—"

"Someone broke into your house?" Blake sat up, setting his empty cup on the coffee table. "When did that happen?"

"It was Tuesday. The kids were in school, and I went out shopping. When I got home, the window in the back door was broken. Someone had come in and ransacked the house."

"What did they take?"

"They broke things. They were definitely in a hurry. They were methodical. They went through everything. But I couldn't find anything missing. I called Peter at work, and of course he was upset, but after thinking about it a moment, he told me not to call the police. That it was best to wait."

"For?"

She shook her head. "I don't know."

Paul's eyes narrowed and he traded a glance with Blake. "You said he met with a city councilman the day before the break-in. Which one?"

"You know," she said, trying to recall the name with the wave of her hand. "The one who's been in all the papers the last few days. Councilman Bullock. The one they say ran off to Mexico with that blonde movie actress."

As they drove back into the city, Paul turned to Blake and said, "I want to go to Councilman Bullock's house. I think we should see what's going on there. Can you get his address?"

"Sure. I can make a call, but it'll probably be just as quick for me to drop by the Glass House." He was referring to the new police administration building downtown near City Hall. "You think Peter O'Keife gave those papers to Councilman Bullock?"

"It sounds like it, doesn't it? O'Keife finds something wrong with the books and goes to the councilman with whatever proof he has."

"And as soon as that happens, the councilman conveniently disappears."

But what connection could there possibly be, Paul wondered, between malfeasance in the construction of the new super highways, the disappearance of a city councilman, and the plan to transform Bunker Hill? "Mrs. O'Keife said the break-in at her house happened on Tuesday. You know, I'm not exactly sure, but I think it was right after that we started to see those headlines about Bullock running off to Mexico in the tabloids."

Paul recalled the story Jeannie had told over dinner at the Biltmore Thursday evening about Bullock and the actress Victoria Lynn, and checked his watch. Both David and Jeannie spent their Saturday mornings downtown helping to put out a monthly homophile magazine. If he was lucky, he could catch her before she left. "If it's okay, I'd like to do a little personal business downtown while you're at the Glass House. If you want, you can drop me off on Hill Street."

"Hill Street? Around Bunker Hill?"

"Right by Angels Flight is fine. I'll meet you there, at the foot of the funicular, say, in an hour?"

Paul was surprised to find other familiar faces from Thursday night's dinner at the Biltmore in the cluttered and crowded office for *ONE Magazine*.

From these two rooms a small staff produced the only national gay publication in the country. Two years before postal inspectors had raided the offices and confiscated the October 1954 issue labeling it obscene under the Comstock Act, which had also been used a generation earlier to criminalize sending birth control information through the mail. Paul had almost laughed when he read the articles considered objectionable, finding them mild as toast—a lesbian love story, a humorous poem, and an advertisement—but he knew how serious this was.

He'd been following the case closely and so far it hadn't been going well. A Federal District Judge had recently ruled the magazine filthy and obscene and calculated to stimulate the lust of the homosexual reader. A decision was now pending before the Ninth Circuit Court of Appeals. If the appeal failed there, which seemed likely, the only recourse was going all the way to the United States Supreme Court, which had never heard a case involving homosexual rights before in the nation's history.

Paul knew the stakes couldn't have been higher. If the suit succeeded, it would force the government to recognize the free speech rights of the homosexual press; if it didn't, it would doom all gay publications to possible seizure and censorship for merely having homosexual content. In the meantime the magazine continued to be published, but under the constant fear of a government crackdown. A lawyer went over every word to try to keep the publication from further postal service raids.

While David and Jeannie were working busily at desks, she on the phone and he apparently playing with the layout for the magazine cover, Pat stood leaning against the towering bookshelves made of wooden crates covering the walls, and Parker Huston lounged in a chair with his legs crossed at the ankles, tapping his wingtips together, his hands resting on his chubby torso. Paul was relieved that

Pat had ditched the awkward garb she had been forced into for dinner at the Biltmore, wearing her usual pants and checkered shirt, but he was also glad she'd added dangly earrings and a necklace to deflect any notions by police she might be attempting to impersonate a man.

Billy was there too, busily filing a stack of papers for David, a bright yellow scarf trailing from around his neck. At least here the boy was safe among friends. Paul reminded himself there was a thing or two he wanted to say to Billy before he left.

"What are you all doing here?" Paul asked, grinning.

"Ah, the Marlboro Man has arrived!" Parker exclaimed. His cheeks were still red and Paul realized that whatever alcoholic blush he'd had the other evening at the Biltmore was becoming a permanent fixture. "I'm taking a class this afternoon," he announced. "All the Heroic Homos in History or some such, I believe."

What had started as cramped offices for the magazine had grown into a meeting place for many purposes. On Saturday afternoons, classes were taught from topics ranging from literature to psychology, anthropology to philosophy, religion to sociology, the first program to offer studies in these fields from a homosexual perspective in the country. On Sundays, the space was used as an ecumenical church. This had been the inspiration for David to come up with the crazy idea of starting a gay synagogue in L.A., one of his wilder notions, which Paul believed would be realized in about a hundred years.

"I'm especially interested to hear about the relationship between Achilles and Patroclus," Parker blathered on. "All the translations we have at the library seem to leave out the juicy details. And what exactly did Caravaggio *do* with all those beautiful boys he painted?"

"Did you ever notice everything that comes out of your mouth is about sex?" David asked, looking up from his work. "You're the horniest librarian I know."

"Because, perhaps, everything *is* about sex." He let out a wistful sigh. "And anyway, pondering these issues makes history come alive, don't you agree?"

Paul nodded greetings at Pat. "Hey, Pat, what are you doing here?"

Pat bounced her back against the bookcase behind her with the nervous energy she always seemed to have, the arms of her checkered shirt crossed at her stomach. "I'm taking Jeannie out to lunch after she's done." Jeannie hung up the phone and waved at Paul.

"I thought you were here to do some heavy lifting, Pat," Parker teased. "Surely there's some furniture that needs to be moved."

"You are a horrible man," Pat scolded, but she couldn't help laughing, "and if I didn't make so much money off you landscaping your yard and doing your gardening once a week, you would feel my wrath."

"You should see her in my yard pushing a wheel barrow," Parker exclaimed. "Those boots! Those torn Levi's! That logger's shirt! Those biceps! That swagger! I called up my mother and told her I had finally found the girl of my dreams."

David tilted his head at Paul. He seemed to have forgiven Paul for the tension the night before, for what he had and hadn't said, but the conversation wasn't finished and the issues weren't forgotten. "Hey, babe, what are you doing here?"

"Actually, I wanted to ask Jeannie about something that came up at dinner Thursday night. You had said that you didn't believe Victoria Lynn had run off with Councilman Bullock..."

Jeannie threw up her hands and exhaled a loud exasperated sigh. "I never should have brought up her name. She's all Pat's been talking about since."

"You know I love you best, but, oh, my God, that woman is a goddess! Have you seen some of the glamour shots of her in the papers this week?" Pat exclaimed dreamily. "Did you see her in *Lightning Strikes Twice*? A goddess!"

"She's as wooden as a totem pole," Parker proclaimed. "But that skin! It's like a creamy satin sheet!"

"Credit the lighting guy for that," Jeannie said knowingly, enjoying her role as a killjoy and wriggling her pert little nose at Pat.

"And that hair!" Parker enthused.

"Peroxide!" Jeannie piped in. "All I can tell you—and I *know*—all those movie stars you think are so beautiful are nothing without the make-up we put on them. Until I get my hands on them, they're perfectly ordinary girls. Me, and the lighting guy, are the real heroes."

A Negro with a striped shirt and khakis poked his head in the doorway from the other room. Paul knew he was one of the founding members of *ONE* but couldn't remember his name. He smiled big white teeth, his eyes dancing, and said, "Sorry, Pat, but from what I've heard, Victoria Lynn likes her women like she likes her coffee... *black* with a little bit of *sugar*."

"Kevin, that sounds like a rumor started by someone who likes his men like he likes his rice... white and steamy," Parker commented. Paul recalled Kevin was a member of the Knights of the Clock, the interracial group that Jeff Dupuis belonged to.

"It ain't no rumor," Kevin said. "Honey, I *saw* that girl last month dancing at Ruby's. And she was in *love* with a sister." Ruby's was a club run by a very large elderly colored woman over in West Adams that catered to Negro lesbians. Big Ruby was known for rescuing young people lost to the street, taking them in and treating them like the children she never had.

"You people ruin all my fun," Pat said in mock despondency.

Paul shook his head as he tried to put the pieces together. If Councilman Bullock had disappeared after receiving the papers Peter O'Keife had given him, how did the actress fit in all this? An actress who was interested in women? If the love nest story had been concocted by the tabloids, what purpose did it serve other than to sell papers? "If you can cut the catty talk for just a second," Paul said, "maybe Jeannie can answer my question. If Lynn is gay, then why has she been connected with the councilman in this supposed love scandal?"

"Ever heard of a marriage of convenience?" Parker asked.

"Look, Paul," Jeannie said, ignoring Parker's comment, "I have no idea. I'm just saying none of it makes sense. That said, I *have* heard she's missing, AWOL from the MGM lot for almost a week. She didn't show up for some publicity stills and the studio is livid. They're threatening her with suspension—if they can find her."

"So maybe she *did* run off with him to Tijuana."

Jeannie gave him a conspiratorial raised eyebrow and hummed the *Dum-de-DUM-DUM* score from *Dragnet*. "Or maybe it was just made to look that way."

David rose from his desk and stretched his arms and yawned. "I'm worn out. Proceed with the revolution without me." He looked at Paul. "You free for lunch?"

"Not today, too much work at the office," Paul said, not sure why he suddenly felt self-conscious saying it. Not sure, either, why he was lying again. Not lying exactly, just not telling the truth. "I'll see you tonight?"

David looked a little disappointed. "I already skipped out on the bar mitzvah of my second cousin this morning, but since you're busy I guess this afternoon I should go to the luncheon at temple. Then it's dinner at my parents'. I'll come over after that."

Before Paul left, he remembered he had one other thing to do. He pointed a finger at Billy, who froze at the filing cabinet. "*You* I want to talk to."

He took Billy into the other room and pinned him against the wall and tugged on his yellow scarf.

"You can wear this in here, but don't wear it outside. And I don't want to see you in that park ever again, do you hear me?"

"What park?" Billy put on his innocent sixteen-year-old blond cherub face.

"Pershing Square. Yesterday. Around ten o'clock in the morning. Do I need to be more specific?"

"Oh."

"Yes, oh. You've been told before to stay away from those places."

"I wasn't doing anything wrong."

"That man you were interested in is a hustler. Do you understand what that means? And he's probably straight. A drifter. He could be a violent criminal. He's not going to be interested in you unless you have five or ten bucks to spare. People like that are dangerous and I want you to stay away."

Billy nodded sulkily, his baby-blue eyes looking hurt, and Paul could only hope he had gotten through to the boy. Back in the front room, he caught David's eye, who got up and walked him to the front door of the office.

After Blake had dropped Paul off across the street from the lower end of Angels Flight, a funicular whose brightly painted train cars chugged up the steep slope between Hill and Olive Street at the top of Bunker Hill, carrying passengers who didn't want to make the climb on foot, he turned the corner, parked the car, and tailed Paul at a safe distance as the prosecutor made his way up the street.

Blake wasn't sure why he was following him, but he had to admit to himself that Paul Winters had been in his thoughts since the night he met him, in a way Blake didn't entirely understand. He certainly thought highly of him and all the deputy district attorney had accomplished, and what a striking and interesting fellow he was. But over his lifetime there had been many others he admired, several commanders in the Navy, his chief back in Milwaukee, his partner on the beat during those ten years, but there was something different about the way he felt about Winters. He realized suddenly that he really just wanted to know him, to be with him, and not just at work. He wanted to be in his confidences, to share things with him, to have Paul Winters feel the same way about him. There was just something about Paul Winters that lifted his spirits and made him want to be around him.

He saw Paul slip into a decrepit building on the next block and quickened his gait. When he reached the doorway and peered through the glass, he spotted Paul's legs at the top of a flight of stairs as the deputy district attorney climbed to the second floor and went down the hall.

Creeping up the stairs, Blake could hear the creak of the old floorboards pursuing Paul as he walked to a door at the end of the hall and went inside. After a moment, Blake followed him, hovering outside the door. It appeared to be some kind of office, but there was no name anywhere. He put his ear against the wood trying to hear the conversation going on inside. People were talking animatedly, but it was impossible to figure out what anyone was saying. Making it even more difficult, the sound of musical scales sung by a rather talentless young girl came from a doorway at the other end of the hall, drowning out the conversation in the office.

A burst of laughter came from inside the room and he almost jumped.

He made his way down the stairs, found a phone booth on the street and called to find out Councilman Bullock's address as he had promised. Then he returned and put his ear to the office door. Still he could only hear muffled conversation.

After a couple of minutes, he heard footsteps coming toward the door and retreated back to the staircase and took a few stairs down, crouching and peering around the banister to see who was coming out.

Blake watched as Paul stepped into the hallway, and was about to descend the stairs and go quickly to his car, when he was stopped dead by the sight of another man who had come to the doorway and was standing in the threshold. He was young and slim, good looking in a Jewish sort of way, with dark wavy hair and a prominent nose, dressed in a polo shirt and khakis.

The two men spoke in intimate tones too quiet for Blake to hear, and something about their whispered confidences set off an alarm in his head and he didn't think he wanted to see more. He was about to turn to go when, to his utter astonishment, he saw Paul lean toward the other man and kiss him on the lips.

Blake felt his stomach roil as he took the stairs down to the street two at a time.

Chapter 8

Jim Blake got in his car and slammed the door. His hand was shaking when he put the key into the ignition.

He had never considered what it would look like, a man kissing another man, and the image filled him with such a sense of upheaval and deep-seated anxiety that he didn't know how to process it. The only response he could latch onto was one of anger, anger at Paul Winters for somehow duping him, for pretending to be someone he wasn't, for being a queer, and anger at himself, because despite his feelings of revulsion and that sickening twisting and turning in his stomach he also had a strange and unsettling pang of being left out, that something was being denied him, and he thought savagely about how handsome the young man was who had been the object of Paul's affection.

When he recalled the intrusive thoughts that had invaded his head since he'd met the prosecutor, it made him even more furious. It had been hard to get the guy out of his head. This had happened to him before, but that time there had been a sense of innocence, of not knowing the consequences; he had only felt the rush of being swept up in something, something that he couldn't control. And for a moment that had been wonderful. But ten years of regret had taught him to fear ever touching that part of himself again, and he had boxed it up and put it on a shelf and never wanted to look at it again.

Blake revved the engine of the Hudson Hornet and pulled into traffic going toward Hill Street.

He had made a mistake coming back to Los Angeles; whatever truce he had naively sought with the past seemed a foolish dream now, and for a moment he considered just getting out now, leaving without a word. He could do it. It would be as simple as buying a train ticket. And then, as he spotted Paul walking down Hill Street toward Angels Flight, he knew that he wouldn't, that he couldn't, that he had to ride this out wherever it took him.

He turned the corner and pulled up in front of the entrance to the funicular, his fingers tapping involuntarily on the steering wheel, and watched through the rear view mirror as Paul stopped on the next block in a knot of pedestrians, waiting for the light to change.

And then, reacting completely from his gut, before Paul had a chance to look up and spot the Hornet, Blake put his foot on the gas and sped away.

It was several hours before Paul got the call. After waiting half an hour at the foot of Angels Flight, not knowing how to contact Blake or what had happened to him at the new police administration building, he'd walked to the District Attorney's Office and began going over case files in his office. There were a few high-profile cases that would dominate his time over the next several months, but he couldn't goad himself to get interested in them. He felt restless, and a little worried, wondering what had become of Blake. He had been thinking about this guy an awful lot since they'd met, and he knew it was a mistake, for so many reasons. And yet he couldn't seem to get him out of his mind.

He jumped when the telephone rang and was relieved to hear Blake's voice on the other end.

"Paul, it's Jim Blake." His voice sounded gruff and sullen. "I'm sorry. Something came up at the Glass House and I couldn't get back to pick you up. When I got free, I called your house but no one answered. Then, even though it's Saturday, I realized maybe you'd gone to your office..."

"Is anything wrong?"

There was a pause, and then, "No. Nothing's wrong."

Paul waited a moment to respond, just listening to the silence over the line, his eyes narrowing with bewilderment. "Well, okay. You got the address?"

"I got it. I can be at your office in ten minutes."

They drove westward through Hollywood with its movie studios and stucco bungalow courts swathed in bougainvillea, the streets lined with gently swaying palms, then cut up to Sunset and the snarl of late Saturday afternoon traffic that reached for miles. The sun settling on the horizon left an orange hue on everything.

"You seem quiet," Paul commented finally. They hadn't said two words since Blake had picked him up at his office downtown.

Blake flicked the remnants of a cigarette out the window. "I was just thinking, that's all."

Paul was puzzled by the change in Blake's demeanor from when he had seen him just hours earlier, wondering if he'd had a hard time at the Glass House getting the information they wanted. There had been no real explanation of what he'd been doing most of the afternoon, and the vice cop had become troubled and moody, and couldn't seem to look Paul directly in the eye. And the chain smoking was worse than before, if that was possible. What the hell was going on?

Paul looked out the window for a while, deciding just to let Blake stew. They passed by Capitol Records in the distance, rising up above lower buildings in the foreground. Built two years before to much fanfare, the cylindrical structure was rumored to have been designed to resemble a stack of 45 r.p.m.s with a stylus on top.

"Did you have any problem finding Councilman Bullock's address?" he asked eventually.

"No," Blake said. Finally he leveled his gaze on Paul as the Hornet slowed to a stop at a red light. "I find it easy to find out things about people."

"Oh," Paul said, shrugging. He knew that there was more to this but chose to let it ride. "So, where are we going?"

"Bullock owns a place in the district he represents just for residency purposes, but he lives in Beverly Hills, just below Sunset on Alta Drive."

Paul knew the area; it was where movie stars lived on wide and quiet tree-lined boulevards lazy with shade, with big houses set back from the street, gardeners forever tooling in the yards, trimming privacy hedges and mowing expanses of Technicolor-green lawn. Just a few blocks northeast lay the stretch of the Strip outside Los Angeles city limits where the favorite haunts of gangsters resided, the nightclubs and the gambling joints, within earshot but just beyond the jurisdiction of the LAPD.

After snaking through the business section of Sunset and entering the lush greenery of Beverly Hills, the Hudson Hornet turned south on Alta Drive and parked a block down.

Jacaranda trees lined the parking strips on both sides of the street, black and scraggly and barren in December, but in spring they would boast the most beautiful lavender blossoms and the neighborhood would come alive with gorgeous color. Then a few weeks later, the flowers would fall in droves on the sidewalks like discarded hopes and dreams, sticking to shoes and automobile hoods and causing an awful mess.

They got out of the car and surveyed the house, standing on the sidewalk. It was one of those old-fashioned white stucco Spanish-style mausoleums from the twenties that everybody was sick of, with black wrought iron ornately protecting the windows, a gently sloping red-tile roof, and sprays of red and pink and white bougainvilleas that climbed the walls like an ardent lover to the balconies on the second floor. Encircling the property was a low squarely-cut hedge inset with a narrow wrought iron gate leading to the front door via a flagstone path, and a wider gate opening on a driveway that curved to a garage behind the house.

The house was silent, the windows dark. They entered through the gate and walked down the path to the front door.

Blake knocked and thumbed the doorbell; neither of them expected an answer. Chimes rang hollowly inside. A moment later he tried the knob, but it was locked. Paul cupped his hands and peered through the stained glass panes on the side of the door.

"It's dark inside. I don't think anyone's there."

Taking a few steps back, Blake said, "If they broke into the O'Keife's house looking for those documents, they may have done the same here. But I don't see any sign of it. Let's try around the back."

They followed the flagstone path around to the back of the house. Even in winter the air was thick with the scent of flowers, jasmine mixed with the smell of pine needles wafting in the breeze.

Paul went to the garage and looked through one of the window panes in the door. "It's a two-car garage, and two cars are in there," he called over to Blake, who was investigating the back of the house. That didn't mean much if Bullock had taken the train to Mexico. But at least they knew he hadn't left in his own automobile. If he'd gone on the train, especially with a famous figure like Victoria Lynn, many people would have recognized them, yet no witness accounts had been mentioned in the papers. When Paul thought about it, he realized the tabloids had never mentioned how the two had arrived at their love nest. Of course, he mused, if the story wasn't a complete fabrication, it was still possible they had taken Lynn's car.

When Paul joined Blake on the stairs to the back door, he found the officer reaching his hand through a broken pane in the door. Shards of glass littered the porch. "Somebody got here first."

Nodding, Paul said, "Whatever they wanted at the O'Keife's house, they didn't get it. So they came here."

"The question is, did they find it?"

Paul and Blake passed through the kitchen and made their way to the front of the house. The place had been trashed, but the house was so large that the ransacking looked like little more than neglectful housekeeping or the aftermath of boisterous teens having a party while their parents were away. If it weren't for a few canisters on the floor in the kitchen, flour and sugar fanning out, a broken lamp lying on the floor in the hall, and a painting leaning against the wall with its canvas torn, calling a maid service might have been a first response to seeing the mess rather than the police.

They entered a sunken living room with red velvet curtains the color of blood hanging from glinting rings on brass rods. The only damage here was a tipped-over pole lamp and a magazine rack on its side. Painted pictures as gaudy as a velvet matador covered the walls, a massive fireplace with a grate big enough to barbecue a slain deer dominating one corner. It was old school, old money, meticulously kept up, and as embalmed as any stiff in the county morgue. The councilman liked to put on a show of tradition, and Paul wondered if that carried into his personal life.

He thought about the flip comment Parker had made. *Maybe it's a marriage of convenience.* He'd never heard any rumors about the councilman, but then, until two nights ago, he'd never heard any rumors about Victoria Lynn, either. Could this have been a show marriage to benefit the both of them? Could it be that Bullock was gay? If that were the case, Paul knew there was only one place in the house to find the evidence.

"I'll check upstairs," he said to Blake, then took the wide staircase rising from the front hall to the second floor. In his years as a prosecutor he had learned that everyone kept things they wanted no one else to see, and always, it seemed, they were hidden where they slept. He entered the master bedroom, flipped on the light switch, and went directly to the closet and slid the mirrored door open.

A row of dark conservative suits presented itself. The inside of the door had a rack with a gaggle of subdued ties. At the far end he noticed one suit was draped with a travel cover. Out of curiosity, Paul unzipped the cover; the suit inside was different than the others, brighter, and on the hanger, a bright red tie. He quickly went through the pockets in the jacket and found a laundry receipt from San Francisco in one and a card in the other. It read:

IF THE POLICE RAID
THIS HOMOSEXUAL
ESTABLISHMENT TONIGHT
READ BACK OF CARD!

118

On the reverse side of the card was a list of instructions, telling the holder not to resist arrest, to only give officers their name and address until consulting an attorney. A 24-hour phone number of the Mattachine Society was listed to call for those who had no attorney or bail bondsman.

The Mattachine Society had been a small homosexual emancipation group founded in the early fifties modeled on a new and radical idea: that gays were a persecuted minority that needed to band together politically to fight for their rights as Negroes and other oppressed groups did. Paul recalled that David had first heard of the organization after a founding member, Dale Jennings, had been arrested by a vice officer in 1952. Instead of pleading down the charge, he went to court before a jury. His lawyer then did something almost no one had done before. He admitted his client was a homosexual but told the jury that the arresting officer was a liar who had followed Jennings home from Westlake Park and forced his way into the defendant's house before calling for backup. The jury deadlocked eleven to one for acquittal, and the charges were dropped.

Excitement over the victory had swelled the membership of Mattachine, and satellite groups popped up all over the state in a brief frenzy of activism and consciousness raising. Success, however, led to the organization's near demise when it was exposed that some of the founding members had previous Communist Party ties; once these members were expunged, a conservative faction took over, scorning activism in favor of soliciting the support of psychologists, ministers and politicians, who were requested to speak on behalf of homosexuals to the rest of society.

David had left the group, bitterly raging that the leaders were courting the very "experts" that were keeping gays down.

Cradling the card in his hand Paul thought about what he had just found. The question was, why did Councilman Bullock have a Mattachine card in his pocket? The suit could have been somebody else's; it was certainly more flamboyant than any of the others. But when Paul checked, he found it was the same size as the rest. Another possibility presented itself, backed up by the laundry receipt. Bullock used the suit when out of town, visiting San Francisco, where he wouldn't be recognized.

This finding made the tabloid headlines screaming of a Tijuana love nest even more unlikely, although, Paul realized, if both Bullock and Victoria Lynn were gay, a marriage of convenience could be valuable for both their careers. But Bullock had left without warning, at a time when he had promised to lead the campaign to stop the destruction of Bunker Hill, leaving his constituents in the lurch. And being seen in the swank nightclubs on Sunset with a starlet on his arm would have provided a more credible front than a disappearing act south of the border.

"You finding anything?" Blake appeared in the bedroom doorway.

Paul almost jumped. "No." He quickly slipped the card back in the suit pocket. "Are you all done down there?"

"Yeah. I'll try the bedroom at the end of the hall," Blake said. He observed Paul a moment before disappearing down the hall.

Once Blake was gone, Paul went through every inch of the closet. There had to be something more. There always was. He checked the shelf above the suits but found only folded sweaters. Nothing on the floor in the back of the closet.

Paul turned from the closet and surveyed the room. First he went through the drawers in the lamp tables flanking the bed. Kleenex, a flashlight, ear plugs. He checked under the bed. Nothing. Throwing back the

120

covers, he slid his arms between the mattress and the box springs. He felt the hard spines of magazines immediately. He pulled one out, then another, and another. Bingo. Beefcake mags.

Paul would have been afraid to have something like this in his house. It was a dead giveaway to police and prosecutors.

He recognized one publication, *Physique Pictorial,* with its cover photo of a scantily clad bodybuilder posing beside fake Greek columns. Thirty-five cents a copy. The publisher and photographer, Bob Mizer, had been convicted and sent to prison in 1947 for selling pictures such as this. His conviction had been overturned several years later on free speech grounds. Paul flipped through the pages. A cowboy with a hat, a handkerchief around his neck, a gun belt and boots—and cut-off denim jeans that had hardly more material than a g-string—was pointing a gun. On another page, clean-cut young men frolicked naked on a beach.

Bullock most likely had picked the magazines up at newsstands, probably when he was out of town on business and the risk of being identified was lower. Of course, it was possible they had been delivered in a plain brown wrapper, but Bullock would have known even that didn't completely protect the recipient from the danger of exposure. The Post Office watched for publications of a homosexual nature and noted the addresses they were sent to, opened personal mail of those suspected of homosexuality, even initiated correspondence in personals columns to entrap those who had placed the ads. The target of such unwanted attention could wake up to find the police or FBI banging on their door with an arrest warrant.

When the sound of Blake's footsteps came from down the hall, Paul quickly—almost frantically—stuffed the magazines back under the mattress and smoothed the covers. He stood up quickly. He didn't have time to ask himself why he was so afraid of being seen with Bullock's magazines, as if he would be tainted by just having them in his hands. He wasn't sure if it was fair not to tell Blake what he had learned—that the tabloid stories about Bullock and Victoria Lynn were likely a sham, that something darker was going on here—but he knew he would not.

"Nothing down the hall." Blake hesitated at the door a moment, assessing the expression on Paul's face before coming into the bedroom. "I think whatever papers O'Keife got from work, either Bullock still has them, or the burglars do."

"I didn't find them here, either," Paul said.

Paul heard something downstairs at the back door and froze. He held up a hand warning Blake, who nodded at him and stood without moving. Footsteps padded from the kitchen then trailed into the other rooms. After a minute, footfalls shook the stairs. The bedroom door, which had been half-closed, was kicked open, banging against the wall.

Lieutenant Falk and Detective Vincent stood in the doorway with their pistols drawn. They didn't seem surprised to find Paul and Blake there.

Falk's steely gray eyes watched Paul balefully, his red face networked with spider capillaries like roads on a map. A toothpick twitched in his mouth. "You were told to stay out of this."

"No, you told me the suicide Thursday night was clean and there was nothing to investigate. Surely you don't think the suicide of a homosexual in Lincoln Heights Jail has anything to do with the disappearance of a city councilman and the ransacking of his home. Or do you know something I don't know?"

"You'll go too far, Winters, and you'll see what it gets you." Falk waved his Remington at them. "You're coming with us. There's somebody who wants to meet you."

The nightclub called The Swallow Inn on Sunset was meant to look like Tara in *Gone with the Wind*, and like the white towering façade on a Hollywood back lot it gracefully hid the truth of what lay beyond its columned porch with a flash of wealth and Southern charm. Paul knew the fancy restaurant boasting New Orleans cuisine and the bar offering mint juleps concealed a gambling joint in the back, just a few blocks outside the Los Angeles city limits and frustratingly out of reach of the LAPD Vice Squad. And any hope of Los Angeles law enforcement working together with the county sheriff was usually snuffed out by regular payoffs in the right pockets of either agency. Paul had heard rumors that live-in party girls were provided for high rollers at the casino around the clock with accommodations for gamblers to spend their winnings on like the Rhett Butler Room with its red velvet wallpaper and four-poster bed and girls to make a man feel like a movie star.

Vincent pulled the unmarked car into the circular drive and stopped at the sweeping front porch. As he and Falk got out into the cool night air, they indicated to Paul and Blake, in the back seat, to do the same. There hadn't been much in the way of conversation in the three minute ride from Bullock's house to the nightclub, but Paul had had time to ponder the significance of their little trip and he didn't like it. He had suspected things were bigger than he had originally imagined, and now he knew it for sure. At least the detectives had put their guns away.

A young Negro valet came up to take the keys to the car, but Vincent waved him away, and said, "Police business, the car stays here."

"But, sir," the valet said, "we can't have you leave your car here. It's against the rules. This is where we bring the cars for customers to pick them up."

Vincent flipped open his badge. Despite his stooped posture, he towered over the valet. "You lay one dirty black finger on that car, and I'll have your ass."

The valet tilted his head and Paul could have sworn the slightest tease of a smile rested on his lips. "But sir," he said politely, gazing up at Vincent, "the LAPD has no jurisdiction here. You see that streetlight?" He pointed down the block. "The city limits end there."

If Falk hadn't caught him by the shoulders, Vincent would have lunged at the young man and torn him apart. "Just give him the damn keys!" Falk wrestled the keys from Vincent, slapped them in the young man's palm, then dragged his partner up the stairs of the expansive porch. Vincent turned, making one last stand, and shouted, "If there's one scratch on that car, I'm coming for you!"

"Welcome to The Swallow Inn, sir," the valet grinned, "I hope your visit is a pleasant one." He slid into the driver's seat and revved up the car, then peeled out in a screech of rubber to the parking area on the side of the establishment.

"Goddamned uppity... getting worse every day," Vincent grumbled, his big nose turning red, his cheeks flushing. "You need to fire that nigger!" he shouted to nobody in particular as the four of them climbed onto the porch and two doormen dressed in gray Confederacy uniforms simultaneously pulled open the double doors for them.

They entered a spacious lobby with red velvet carpet leading to a wide staircase. On one side, a busy restaurant catering to finely coutured local hipsters and somewhat more staidly dressed tourists getting a taste of the world of the demimonde. On the other, a sprawling bar with paneling of rich dark mahogany.

As they passed the hat-check station and a counter selling papers and a bank of telephone booths, a cigarette girl approached them in Southern Belle garb with a tray of her wares and a tired smile. "Any cigarettes tonight, gentlemen?"

"Scram," Vincent said gruffly, shooing her aside, still grumpy from his scuffle with the valet. He straightened his thinning hair as best he could.

"You two wait in the bar. Vincent, keep them company. I'll be right back." Falk left them and took the wide red velvet staircase two stairs at a time.

In the bar Paul and Blake found seats at a table, while Vincent paced back and forth, still grousing. Almost immediately Paul spotted a mahogany door toward the back of the bar, and a dapper middle-aged man knocking on it. He conferred a moment with the man who answered, then was allowed to enter. The casino, Paul thought.

"If that nigger so much as spits on my car, he's a dead man," Vincent went on.

"Just go check on the goddamned car," Paul said through his teeth. "We aren't going anywhere."

As Paul signaled for a waitress to come and take their order, Vincent glared at them suspiciously, then stalked back toward the entryway. When the waitress, a young woman in dyed blonde hair and full make-up, approached, Paul said, "We were itching to do a little gambling tonight. What would it take to get us inside?" He slipped a folded ten dollar bill into her hand.

"You look like cops," she said bluntly.

"I'm an accountant with Myers, Myers and Silverstein over on Wilshire," Paul said. "This is my brother-in-law from Minnesota."

"I'm a farmer," Blake said, looking positively corn-fed. He gave her a smile and a lock of his hair fell down on his forehead as if on cue, and Paul was struck again by what a beautiful man he was. "And I'd really like to have some fun while I'm in your town."

She batted her eyelashes under his gaze. "Well," and here she whispered conspiratorially, "we're not supposed to say. But if you go to the door and say Mel sent you, they'll let you in." She took Paul's ten and slid it down between her breasts.

They waited for their drinks to arrive before sauntering over to the door which had a peephole like a Prohibition era speakeasy. The man at the door didn't seem particular about letting them in once Paul uttered the magic phrase, and they found themselves in a dim smoky room crowded with gamblers, mostly men, but several with a girl at their side who probably wasn't their wife. A roulette wheel spun in the center surrounded by poker and blackjack tables headed by dealers with the steely gaze of the coyotes in the hills above the casino.

Beyond an arched doorway Paul noticed a hallway studded with a series of doors, and he wondered if this was the site of the famed bedrooms for high rollers who wanted more than just a girl on their arm. As if to prove his theory wrong, there was a flash of light in the hall and a sudden commotion as three big men in expensive suits converged on a man with a camera who had been peering into one of the rooms as a waiter with an empty tray in his hand exited, quickly closing the door behind him.

One of the bouncers grabbed the camera, yanked the back open, and unspooled the roll of film, exposing it to the light, while the two other bruisers took the photographer in hand and shoved him through the casino toward the front door with the doorman standing guard.

"Beat it!" one of the bouncers barked.

"Hey, I'm just a guy trying to make a living."

The bouncer who had grabbed the camera now tossed it at the photographer, who scrambled to catch it.

"Make it somewhere else."

Once the photographer had been ejected Paul returned his attention to the closed door in the hall, staring and trying to understand the meaning of what he'd seen in the instant before the waiter had swung the door shut. It was not a gaudy fantasy room for sexual encounters as he had suspected, but a tastefully furnished private dining room set out of the way for discreet get-togethers out of the public eye.

There was no doubt in his mind that he'd spotted Pritchard Sondergaard in his white linen suit sitting at a table dining alone with a woman. No doubt that the woman was one of the most beautiful he had ever seen. Platinum blonde. Regal. Statuesque. Poured into a shimmering black dress that accentuated every curve.

And no doubt that the woman was Victoria Lynn.

Chapter 9

Paul and Blake were back at their table in the bar when Falk finally came trotting down the red velvet stairs. He looked both ways as he approached them, as if searching for someone.

"Where the hell is Vincent?"

"I guess he had car trouble," Blake said, taking a sip of his tequila.

"They want you upstairs. Now." Falk hiked his thumb toward the stairs. When both men began to rise from the table, he shook his head. "No, not you," he said to Blake, then gave Paul a nod. "Just you."

Paul rose, then shrugged at Falk, waiting for directions for where to go upstairs.

"Just go up. They'll find you."

He exchanged a glance with Blake, then left the bar and climbed the wide staircase. On the second floor a meticulously dressed short and stocky man in a sharkskin suit nodded to him and escorted him under chandeliers to wide double doors at the end of a hall of gilt mirrors. Paul grinned to himself, realizing the rumors he'd heard about the man he was about to meet were true. Barely reaching a height of five three, Mel Fischer was fabled to surround himself with underlings of similar or lesser stature. It was one way to become a big man.

Paul entered a spacious office with closed doors on both sides leading, he supposed, to inner offices. A man puffing on a cigar sat behind a large desk in the center talking quietly on a phone, framed from behind by big windows black with night that looked out into the landscape behind the building, a craggy scrub-covered hill that rose nearly as steeply as a cliff. A few henchmen sat in the corners of the room, alert and ready to do their boss's bidding, and, of course, to shield the big guy from assassination attempts, an occupational hazard of the business they were in.

"Deputy District Attorney Paul Winters," the man behind the desk said, hanging up the phone and chomping on what appeared to be a half-eaten cigar. "I'm the owner of this establishment. Mel Fischer."

Paul was aware of his reputation. Mel Fischer was fat and balding with a permanent patina of sweat on his forehead. In another era he would have been a tailor in Brooklyn like his father and his grandfather before him, but the mid-twentieth century had offered him opportunities his forefathers never dreamed of. He had taken over Mickey Cohen's territory when the racketeer went to prison several years before on tax fraud charges, but was smart enough to learn from his predecessor's mistakes, and had enough legit businesses on the side to cover for his numbers running, gambling, call girl services, and other illegal activity.

He gestured for Paul to take a seat in a plush upholstered chair in front of the desk. Paul could tell Fischer's own chair had been jacked up to give him height behind the desk and the diminutive mobster's feet were probably dangling in the air under the desk like a child's. But, as Paul had learned a long time ago, the world of gangsters on the Strip was not so different from the sphere of the movie stars in the Hollywood studios a few miles to the east: image was everything.

Paul folded his arms after sinking into the cushions. "You had me brought here, now what do you want?"

"I thought it was time for you and me to get acquainted. I have found that when misunderstandings occur it's because people don't talk out their differences, and then someone gets hurt. Sometimes they get hurt very badly."

"If you think I'm afraid of you, I'm not. I just sent one of your kind to life in prison this week, in case you missed the papers. And his gambling joint was a hell of a lot bigger than this, and his decorator a hell of a lot more original."

Fischer laughed sharply and chewed on his stogie. "You think you made a big score sending Smiling Willy to San Quentin for life, don't you? But the truth is, someone had elbowed in on his territory before the papers hit the pavement celebrating your victory."

"Still," Paul said, returning the laugh, "there's some satisfaction in knowing that murderer will be spending the rest of his life in a cage, isn't there?"

After appraising him a moment, Fischer stubbed out the butt of his soggy cigar. "You don't ask the right questions, Mr. Deputy District Attorney. You should have asked who took Willy's place."

"I suppose that was you?" Paul shrugged to let him know he wasn't impressed. "Well, enjoy it while it lasts."

"What's that supposed to mean?"

"Okay, you're a big man. I get it. Until Mickey wants his territory back. Then you're just Mickey's boy again."

If Fischer had been taken down a notch he didn't show it. He opened a cigar box on the desk, took one, and nodded to Paul to do the same. Paul remained still in his chair.

After biting off the end, Fischer lit up in a cloud of smoke and observed Paul balefully. "You ain't heard. Mickey's done. He found Jesus. He ain't the same man."

"If you say so." Mickey Cohen, who had been a protégé of Bugsy Siegel in the forties, and the most infamous and flamboyant gangster since, had been released from prison a few years before insisting he had reformed and seemed more interested lately in developing his celebrity than returning to the rackets. Paul wondered how long that would last.

A gray Persian cat streaked across the carpet and jumped on the mobster's lap. His thick plume of a tail twitched in Fischer's face. He began to stroke the cat's back, rubbing firmly on his rear end, which stuck up in the air. "Everything you want to learn about human nature, all you have to do is look at a cat. Mickey here, he jumps on my bed at six in the morning because he wants to be fed, and he doesn't let up. Walks over my head, back and forth, if he has to. And then he meows like crazy at night when he wants to get out to screw some pretty alley cat."

"If you're suggesting all anyone wants is food and sex, that's not a very original thesis."

"That's not what I'm saying. *Want, want, want*. That's all there is. Desire fulfilled, or unfulfilled. It could be food. It could be sex. It could be power or money. The only thing that makes people different from each other is that some people go after what they want and others don't."

"You sure you're not talking about greed?"

"I'm talking about human nature, Mr. Winters. Don't fight it."

"Okay, thanks for the philosophy lesson. But you haven't answered my question. You had me brought here, what do you want?"

Before Fischer could answer, a side office door opened and a little old man appeared. He was balding with spectacles, in a drab suit that didn't fit over his potbellied waist very well. He stopped abruptly, the expression of concentration on his face turning to surprise upon the realization that Mel Fischer wasn't alone. Fischer shook his head subtly and the old man abruptly turned on his heel and was gone, the door quickly clicking closed behind him. It all happened in the blink of an eye, in Paul's peripheral vision, but not fast enough for him not to catch a glimpse of what was in the man's hands: a stack of papers six inches high bundled with a fat red rubber band with a few blue folders on the top.

If nothing else came from this encounter with Fischer, at least Paul now knew what had become of the Department of Transportation documents that had apparently gone from Peter O'Keife's hands to Councilman Bullock and finally to the backroom accountant of a Sunset Strip gangster.

Fischer leaned forward at his desk. "I want you to butt out and mind your own goddamned business."

"So your house of cards doesn't fall? You've already got what you wanted, now that the city council has voted to sell Bunker Hill to the highest bidder. I just don't know how you expect to hide all the bodies you've left behind."

As Fischer glowered at him, the cat jumped down and rubbed his chin against the edge of the desk, then soft-toed toward Paul, who got up from his chair and gave him a few strokes on the back before strolling over to the windows and gazing outside into the darkness. He stared at nothing for a moment, then a movement below him caught his eye. On a veranda on the floor below, Victoria Lynn stood alone, leaning against the railing, staring out at the same darkness, the breeze ruffling her satin hair.

"Why are you holding Victoria Lynn here?"

Fischer swiveled in his chair toward Paul, who turned away from the window to face him. Paul smiled when he saw he'd been right: Fischer's feet dangled six inches from the floor.

Contemplating his cigar, Fischer said, "The starlet, you mean? We're not holding anyone. She's free to go as she pleases. I hardly think dining at one of the finest restaurants on the west coast constitutes being *held*."

"It is if she can't leave. It is if she's being forced to hide away in one of the rooms of your brothel so people will believe a tabloid story."

"If I had a brothel, which I don't, there would be worse places to be. I run a class joint. But talk to her if you'd like, she'll tell you."

"I will. Are we done here?"

"As long as we understand one another."

"Without a doubt."

He went for the door. Fischer's henchmen began to rise from their chairs, looking for guidance from their boss; when he nodded, they eased back in their seats. Paul opened the door and hesitated there, before he went out.

"Thank you for bringing me here. It answers the question I had about exactly who the architects of this conspiracy are. Now I know that you're involved too."

As he strode down the mirrored hall, he remembered the accountant hidden away in the adjoining office, and the only other question on his mind at the moment was how he was going to get his hands on those papers.

At the bottom of the stairs Paul hesitated for a moment while he made up a plan. He walked into the wide entrance hall and went directly to a phone booth and made a call. Then he returned to the bar and sat next to Blake at their table.

When he was done explaining what had happened upstairs, he glanced around and asked, "What happened to Falk?"

"He went out after Vincent. But, to tell you the truth, I think their job for the night is done. Lackey bastards."

"Pritchard Sondergaard is going to be paged in a minute to take a phone call," Paul said. "Once he comes out I'd like you to corner him and keep him busy for a few minutes. Play drunk and sloppy if you want to, just stop him from going back into his private dining room in the casino."

"Sure. But what's going on?"

"The woman he's with is the one all the tabloids are claiming is down in Tijuana with Councilman Bullock."

"Victoria Lynn."

Paul realized with a spear of guilt that he had been holding out on his partner in this investigation because of the rumors about the actress and what he'd found in Bullock's bedroom, and how unfair it was to let his discomfort with the subject allow him to keep Blake in the dark.

Paul nodded. "Here he comes."

The maitre d' was escorting Sondergaard through the bar and into what was apparently an office to take the call.

"He's going to find out soon enough nobody's on the line," Paul said. "That's where you come in."

Paul strode to the door to the casino, gave the password, then made his way to the private dining room and went in without hesitation, quickly closing the door behind him. He went around the table to the glass paneled doors leading to a veranda. He could see Victoria Lynn's hair gleam against the night as she leaned on the railing outside.

"Miss Lynn?"

She didn't turn. Instead, she spoke as if to the night. "What is it?" When he didn't answer at first, she turned toward him and registered surprise, apparently because he wasn't one of Mel Fischer's thugs. She tilted her head at him, as if she knew the soft light coming through the doors from the dining room would cast a lovely glow on her features. Her low-cut gown sliced a sharp V across the exquisite curve of her milk-white breasts and Paul could see why Pat and so many fans were enamored of her. She

134

was even more beautiful now than when he'd seen her on the silver screen.

"My name is Paul Winters. I'm a Deputy District Attorney. I'd like to talk to you."

She nodded, and something that seemed akin to hope came across her face. "I know who you are. I've seen you in the papers."

"I want to help you, and if I'm right you need help. But I've got a lot of questions." He glanced back toward the dining room. "And I don't think we've got a lot of time."

She gazed beyond his shoulder, then said. "Go ahead. I'm not going anywhere."

"I need to know how this whole scandal in the tabloids came about. Obviously you're not snuggling in your Tijuana love nest with Councilman Bullock, but there are people in this city that want everybody to think so."

"The funny thing is that I've never even met him."

"I guess they figured the two of you make an attractive couple. The photographs in the tabloids certainly make you look happy together."

"Everybody knows a doctored photo when they see one, but they believe anyway. It's like the movies. An awful lot of lies but it makes everybody feel better in the dark." She smiled wanly. "Do you have a cigarette?"

He took two out and lit both of them, and they stood for a minute assessing one another.

"What do they have on you?"

"Who says they do?"

"They're hiding you away so people will believe Councilman Bullock missed the vote on razing Bunker Hill because you two had run off together. The question for me is: where is he since he's clearly not with you? He's missing, so is a cop who got snoopy, and so is an accountant who took some papers that are now in the hands of Mel Fischer's accountant. So, again, my first question for you is, what do they have on you?"

"Nothing," she said. But her cool expression began to crumble and she covered her face with her beautifully sculpted hands, her nails long and red and as carefully manicured as a rich man's garden.

"Then I can't help you."

She pulled her hands away from her cheeks and appraised him with worried eyes for a long time, making up her mind. She let out a deep breath, and for one brief moment her face became a mask of disappointment and Paul wondered if she wasn't older than everyone thought she was. "I was one of Brenda's girls." She waited for his response, and when he didn't offer one, asked, "Does that surprise you?" She met his gaze directly, almost boldly, then looked away from him. "I had just gotten into town and I didn't have a dime. I was a kid, really. I didn't do it long. Just long enough for them to have evidence to use against me."

Brenda Allen was a call girl who had made herself over in the late forties into a successful madam and had been the center of a scandal several years before when she testified before a grand jury regarding payoffs she had made to the LAPD in order to protect her racket. Unlike other proprietresses who set up establishments for prostitution, Allen had only a telephone exchange, which johns would call to request a lady of their liking, and would be told on what street corner to pick her up. Her girls were always dressed in mink and finery, and nobody suspected a respectably dressed woman of any impropriety as she waited demurely on the street for her ride.

"That was a long time ago, what, five, six years?"

She gave him a wry, sad smile, and he realized why so many men had longed for her wide, full lips. "Longer than that." Her tone became sardonic. "But you have to

136

remember, five years ago I was growing up on a wheat farm in Washington State, or at least that's what my studio bio says."

He thought about the gossip he'd heard this afternoon down at the *ONE* office about her being spotted at the colored lesbian bar Ruby's. "Is that all they've got?"

Her eyes darted away from him. "Apparently, it's enough."

"What's your connection with Pritchard Sondergaard?"

She laughed bitterly. "He's my lawyer. Can you believe it? He's the one I hired on advice from the studio to take care of me."

Paul remembered that Sondergaard was rumored to be at the beck and call of Hollywood moguls when their stars got into trouble. He wondered if some scandal sheet had gotten pictures of Lynn with one of her colored girls and the studio needed the whole story shut down.

She took a drag on her cigarette and exhaled through her nose. "Do you know what the name Sondergaard means?"

"No."

"I don't either, but it should mean *octopus*. He has his tentacles everywhere, in every pot, and there's no one he doesn't know."

"And how is he protecting you?"

"He promised me once this all blows over, everything can go back to normal. If I lie low and let people believe I'm off in Mexico with Councilman Bullock, all the stuff they have on me will go away. I just have to play ball."

Paul believed her story and suspected Victoria Lynn was just a pawn being used for the time being, but he didn't think any of the players in this game would think twice about sacrificing her for their own gain. "You may know too much, Victoria. They may not let you go."

"But I don't know anything!" she cried.

"Maybe not, but their story about your love nest with Councilman Bullock falls apart if you're seen around town."

"They said if I just laid low for a while…"

"Don't you see they can never allow you to answer any questions from the press? If they do, the scam they're perpetrating crumbles. They have to shut up everybody who can bring them down. I'm surprised they haven't done it to you already. People are getting killed and people are going missing because of this. Don't you understand what danger you're in? Walk out of here with me right now. I'll make sure you're protected. Testify against them. The District Attorney's Office will be behind you."

She shook her head and tears came to her eyes. "No, I can't. There's something else, something I…"

He grabbed her by the wrist. "You think I care about what you were doing at Ruby's? Didn't you hear me? People are dying and people are disappearing. I don't want you to be next."

Victoria Lynn shook her head and pulled away from him. "I can't go. They'd kill me if I did. My testimony wouldn't mean anything. Do you know what Mel Fischer is like? If I crossed him there'd be nowhere I could run that he wouldn't follow me."

"We'd have you under police protection."

"Do you realize how funny that is?"

Considering who had brought him here, her point was not lost on him. Paul thought a moment. "You mentioned Fischer. Have you met him? Have you been up there? Up to his offices?"

"He likes to meet the movie stars who come slumming to his nightclub," she said tartly.

"Look, in his offices his accountant has a stack of papers with a few blue folders, all wrapped up in a thick red rubber band. Did you ever see them?"

She shook her head. "When Mel met me, that wasn't the kind of business he was interested in. Why, what are they?"

"I'm not sure. But they could be documented proof of a conspiracy. I've got to get my hands on those papers. I need them to bring these people down. If I can figure out how to get them, I might be able to save you."

Before she could respond, Paul heard Pritchard Sondergaard's haughty voice as the portly attorney breezed out onto the veranda.

"Mr. Winters, fancy meeting you here. If you had been honest, and asked to speak to my client, rather than playing little games with me, I would have told you that Miss Lynn has no interest in speaking with you and if you have any questions for her in the future they are to go through me." He paused, turning to Victoria, and added, "Isn't that true, Miss Lynn?"

She turned away from him without answering and looked into the darkness, her hands clutching the veranda railing.

He slid his arm around her waist and she shivered. "Isn't that true, Miss Lynn?"

"Yes," she said in almost a whisper, without turning her head.

Sondergaard smiled at Paul. "That's your cue to leave."

Paul hesitated. "Miss Lynn…"

She shook her head, staring into the night. "Just go."

But just as he exited through the door, Victoria Lynn turned her head and caught Paul's eye. The expression on her face was one of helplessness, and he thought she looked like the loneliest little girl in the world.

Paul found Blake waiting for him at the table in the bar and they walked out together. Falk and Vincent had disappeared, but Paul figured they'd earned their payoffs for the night, and if they wanted more, there were plenty of ways for corrupt cops to make a dime along the Sunset Strip on a Saturday night.

Alta Drive in Beverly Hills, where they had left the Hudson Hornet in front of Bullock's house, was a ten minute walk. They crossed to the south side of Sunset and as they strode briskly down the street Paul and Blake put together the pieces of the puzzle that they knew so far.

"This is big," Paul said, shaking his head ruefully. "This conspiracy involves half the leaders of the city council, as well as Pritchard Sondergaard and a member of the mob. They're all in league on this."

Blake nodded. "They must have stolen money from the super highway projects. That's what Peter O'Keife discovered in those documents. That's why they had to get rid of him."

"And that's why they had to kill Charles Turner. He was in the same cell with O'Keife. Turner must have mentioned to Pritchard Sondergaard when he called him asking for representation Thursday night that his cell mate also worked at the Department of Transportation. It was too big a risk. O'Keife might have told his co-worker what he had uncovered."

Again Blake nodded as they turned down Alta Drive. "So Sondergaard called Falk and ordered him to get rid of Turner and make it look like a suicide."

"Falk and Vincent couldn't just take Turner out and shoot him. He had been booked—there was a record of his arrest—unlike O'Keife."

"You think Bullock, O'Keife and Sergeant Hollings are all dead? Killed by Falk and Vincent?"

"Probably. But I would have said the same of Victoria Lynn, and she ended up alive in a Sunset Strip gambling joint."

"If the others are dead, where did they bury them? It's not easy to hide a body. Let alone three."

They passed a dark patch on the sidewalk where no streetlights glowed.

Out of the periphery of his vision Paul saw the branches of a nearby hedge jump, and heard the sound of rustling leaves and the sudden scuff of shoes on the pavement close behind them. Before he could spin around or warn Blake, he felt a jarring blow to the back of his head and found himself collapsing forward, falling on all fours on the sidewalk.

He heard a terrible hollow thud and could sense Blake going down beside him, but all he could see in the darkness were his hands splayed before him on the sidewalk as he struggled to stay conscious. He flipped on his back quickly as a defensive move to face his assailant, his head swimming, his arms raised in protective position with his hands locked at his elbows to block further blows. Two men stood above them, dark silhouettes in hats, their faces obscured by handkerchiefs, but it didn't take a genius to figure out who they were. The blur of a sap came at Paul with brutal force, glancing off his raised forearms and sending shock waves of pain all the way to his shoulders.

Close by he could hear the swift strike of a sap, and turning his head, he saw that Blake was lying face-down on the sidewalk, unable to get up, trying to crawl away, as his attacker repeatedly brought the weapon down on his back and head.

Paul knew the assailants weren't planning to kill them when one of them took him by the hair and spoke in his ear.

"Why can't you learn to just keep your nose out of other people's business?"

The voice was muffled through the handkerchief mask, and Paul couldn't be sure, but there was little doubt in his mind that it was the voice of Lieutenant Falk. At least he didn't have to wonder anymore where the homicide detectives had disappeared to.

Then the two attackers turned and ran into the night.

Paul crawled over and found Blake sprawled on the pavement, breathing hard.

"Can you get up?"

Blake nodded, but he didn't move.

"I think so," he said finally.

When Paul helped him to rise to his feet, he saw that Blake's face was bloody.

"Let's get in the car. Come, lean on me. I need to have your keys."

He assisted Blake getting into the passenger seat then went around the Hudson Hornet and got in the driver's side. He started the car and drove north on Alta Drive toward Sunset.

"I'm going to take you to the hospital." Paul could taste blood in his mouth but he wasn't sure where it had come from. He ran his tongue over his teeth and they all seemed to be there.

"No…" Blake said, "no, just… drive."

Paul turned west on Sunset then drove far up into the hills.

Chapter 10

He pulled to the side of a winding blacktop road on the rim of a bluff somewhere in the hills and cut the engine. Beyond the hanging branches of a weeping willow rising from the edge of the drop-off, the lights of the city spread out before them. The nearest house was up at the next curve and as dark as the night around them. They sat for a while, not saying anything, just catching their breath, gazing into the distance.

Finally, when their breathing slowed to an easy unison, Paul looked over and said, "You're still bleeding."

"I have an emergency medical kit in the trunk."

Neither moved for a moment, then Blake took the keys from the ignition, opened the door, and stiffly got out of the car. Paul hesitated a moment, then, without knowing quite why, got out too and met Blake at the back of the Hornet. The stars hung above them sharp and bright like they never did in the city, and there was a subtle smell of jasmine in the breeze that gently rattled the leaves in the trees and brush on the hilltop.

Blake slid the key in the slot, popped the trunk, and found a metal box. In the dim light from the bulb glowing in the trunk lid, Paul could assess his companion's injuries better. The left side of his lower lip was thick and purple, his hair disheveled, and blood that hadn't yet dried ran from each nostril and pooled in the lines between his nose and mouth.

"You're a mess."

"Yeah, I kind of figured."

Closing the trunk, Blake made his way around his side of the car at the edge of the precipice, but instead of getting in the front, he opened the back door. When he caught Paul's questioning glance, he said, "I think there's more room back here."

Paul nodded and went around the other side and got in the back too. When they were settled Paul took the metal box and opened it, examining what was inside. He found a bottle of hydrogen peroxide and a small towel.

"You don't look so good yourself," Blake said, watching him. "Sure you're all right?"

"Oh," Paul said, self-consciously straightening his hair, which had been sticking to his forehead, "I guess I'm okay." The back of his head hurt, but he'd felt back there and found no blood. He had a slight headache, but the palms of his hands hurt more than anything else where they'd been scratched by the rough cement surface of the sidewalk when he'd been bludgeoned down on all fours.

Paul tried to clean his hands the best he could, splashing the hydrogen peroxide on them and rubbing his palms together. Then he wetted the towel and leaned toward Blake. Blake hesitated a brief moment before leaning forward and letting Paul begin to wipe the blood away from his nose. He winced when the hydrogen peroxide touched his skin, and for a second the smell made his stomach turn.

"You okay?" Paul asked.

"I think so. It stings a little."

"I'm almost done." He folded the towel, wetted a clean area, and continued. When he was finished, he went through the contents of the aid kit. "Not much I can do for the lip. I guess if we had ice…"

He stared at Blake for a moment, then glanced away.

"What is it?"

"Oh, nothing."

"No, tell me."

"It's just… your eyes, they change color in the light. I can't tell what color they really are."

"What color are they now?"

"I don't know. Black, maybe."

Blake leaned in and to Paul's surprise kissed him on the mouth. It wasn't a gentle, preliminary kiss, but brutal, a hard slap in the face, an accusation. They stared at each other in stunned speechlessness, as if Blake was as knocked off balance by what had occurred as Paul, and then Blake kissed him again, rough still, but long and slow, and this time Paul responded, with his tongue, with his arms around Blake's broad shoulders. The first aid kit slipped off his lap and fell to the floor, its contents scattering.

While still kissing him, Blake loosened his own tie, fumbled with his buttons, and yanked off his shirt. Paul could smell an earthy, musky scent coming off him, the hair on his chest and armpits black masses in the darkness of the back seat. Paul followed suit, dropping his shirt on the floor. And then they were feeling each other's bare chests, running their fingers through the hair, kissing all the while, kissing hard, tongues intertwined.

Paul pulled his mouth away, his hands cradling Blake's chin.

"Your lip," he said quietly, "does it hurt?" He bent forward and gently, ever so gently, took Blake's bulging lower lip into his mouth, his tongue caressing the hard swollen lump. When he was done, Blake covered his face in kisses and Paul saw in the dim light there were tears on his cheeks.

"I'm not sure what I'm doing," Blake admitted, his voice hardly a whisper. He was taken aback by the gentleness of Paul's lips and embarrassed by his own emotion. He wiped his cheeks with the backs of his hands. "I'm not sure why we're here."

"Come," Paul said. "Lay beside me."

Moving to the edge of the seat, Blake allowed room for Paul to recline on his back, and then Blake lay at his side, partially on top of him. Blake's head rested on Paul's chest. With the tip of his head against the back door on the bluff side of the road, Paul could see the lazy cascade of weeping willow branches through the back side and rear windows, and beyond, the night sky.

"I can see the stars from here." He stroked Blake's hair as they lay there. "You know, for once, your hair actually has an excuse to be falling forward onto your forehead, and this is the one time it doesn't."

"Go figure," Blake said. He laid his big hand on Paul's chest, and the expanse of his fingers and thumb was wide enough to span both nipples.

They were quiet for a while, then Paul said, "Something happened to you, didn't it? That guy you told me about... in the war. You've done this before, haven't you?"

Blake was silent a long time before he answered. He had never spoken about it to anyone in the ten years since it had happened. It had been on his mind so long, every moment relived so many times, that now he didn't know where to begin. He opened his mouth to speak, but nothing came out.

"What was his name?" Paul asked, as if he understood how difficult it was for Blake.

"Jack Spencer."

"You met him in the Navy."

Blake nodded into the hair on Paul's chest. "We were friends, great friends. We went through a lot together, you know, overseas."

"I was too young to go. You saw action?"

146

Blake nodded, but he didn't elaborate, except to say, "Okinawa." He hesitated, as if he couldn't put it into words, then said, "It was after the war ended, something, uh, happened between us. I mean, demobilization was in progress and most soldiers were getting their discharge papers. But we were still in the service, stationed here in L.A., waiting to get out. It tore our hearts out that we wouldn't be seeing each other anymore. We had been through so much, and we'd been so young. There's a bond that forms, you know, between men who saw the kind of things we saw. Anyway, his family had a ranch in Barstow, and he was going back. I guess I didn't have any reason to go back, but Wisconsin was where I was from, so that's where I was headed. I guess something just kind of came over us." He fell silent again.

"Where did it happen?" Paul asked, still playing with the curls on Blake's head. "Where did you get caught?"

Blake swallowed. "It was behind the mess hall. There was a clean-up job we were doing. It was dark, after dinner, and nobody else was around. Jack just bent over suddenly, like somebody had hit him with a sandbag in the stomach. But when I approached him, there were tears in his eyes and I could see he was crying. I just took him in my arms and he wailed, his whole body shaking. And then…"

Paul waited for him to go on, and when he didn't, Paul asked quietly, "Then what happened?"

"He told me he loved me. He told me he wanted to be with me for the rest of his life. I held him in my arms and I… I told him I loved him too." He was in a distant place when he continued, his voice far away. "And then we were against the back wall of the mess hall, behind a dumpster and he was kissing me and unbuttoning my shirt and pulling my pants down to my ankles. And then he was on his knees taking me in his mouth." He paused, and his tone

147

changed. "If I hadn't looked up just then, I probably wouldn't have known who reported us. But a private who I barely knew had just turned the corner of the mess hall and was standing there in the darkness watching us. I think I blinked my eyes and he was gone. I wasn't even sure if what I'd seen was real."

"And then they came for you?"

"Jack first. The next day, a hot sticky afternoon. They took him into custody and I didn't know what they had done with him. I kept hoping it was something else, some other reason they had arrested him, but I guess I knew it was all over." When he spoke now his voice came out very quietly. "They arrested me late that night. I learned later they had interrogated Jack for nine hours. I had hoped that we could get out of it by just denying it. It was dark. It would be our word against his. You can't ruin two people's lives based on what someone says he saw for a moment in the dark. But it wasn't our word against that private. In the end, Jack confessed, he broke down and told them everything. He told them we were in love with each other. When he couldn't take it anymore, he brought me down with him. It would mean a dishonorable discharge for being a queer. Every time you applied for a job..."

Paul held him tightly, stroking his hair.

Blake raised his head, and there was something plaintive in his voice. "I couldn't understand how he could do it, I still don't. I mean, how could he do that to me, after he'd told me he loved me?"

Paul ran his fingers across the rough stubble on Blake's jaw. "You can't know what happened to him that night. You can't know how alone he was. Things happen to people in situations like that. Sometimes people do things they never thought they were capable of."

"I denied everything. I don't think they wanted to believe it of me. I'd received two Purple Hearts. I said that

148

Jack had made a spectacle of himself bothering me and I'd rebuffed every pass. The private was mistaken in the dark; Jack had come on to me and I'd pushed him away. In the end, after a night of interrogation, they let me go. They believed me. When I went to the barracks, Jack was packing his things. He took me into a corner and he told me that none of it mattered. That nobody would even care after the war what a dishonorable discharge was. That we could be together. That I could come with him to Barstow." Blake shook his head. "I told him he was crazy. I told him I meant I loved him as one soldier loves another. Not... not like... I told him he had ruined everything. I told him I could never love him. I told him I never wanted to see his fucking face again."

"What happened then?"

"He got a look on his face, a look I didn't know how to interpret. And then he went quickly to his locker and took something out. Maybe I knew what it was. Maybe I was just so angry with him that I didn't care. Maybe I was just so afraid. He went into the restroom, and a moment later, I heard a gunshot." He began to shake and he was crying in Paul's arms.

"I'm sorry," Paul said in his ear and held him until he quieted down.

After a while Blake raised his head and wiped his face. "I cared more about him than I've ever cared about anybody. I know now I loved him more than I've ever loved anybody."

They heard the whoosh of a car go by down the road, its headlights reflecting in a quick flash on the car ceiling before everything went dark and silent again, and once more they were alone in the night.

"I lied to you," Blake said. "About where I was this afternoon."

"I thought there was something you weren't telling me. You seemed different when you finally came to pick me up. Where did you go this morning when you were supposed to meet me at Angels Flight? You didn't go to the Glass House to get Bullock's address, did you?"

"No. I just got in the car and drove. All the way to the ocean. And then, I don't know, I just walked for a long time along the beach."

"I don't understand."

"I saw you with someone. A man."

Paul's body stiffened involuntarily with that primal fear that never went away, the fear of having his private life revealed and losing everything. He trusted Blake and yet he heard wariness in his own voice. "Where?"

"I followed you. After I dropped you off downtown, I tailed you. You went into a building on Hill Street. After you were done, you stepped out into the hall with him."

Paul closed his eyes momentarily, remembering. Now he understood Blake's aggressive kiss when they'd first gotten into the back seat, the kiss that felt like an accusation. "That was David. We've been seeing each other."

"Is he… like…"

"My boyfriend? Yeah, he's my boyfriend."

"Are you… are you in love with him?"

Paul hesitated. "I don't know. He—David's really the best person I know. But he scares me and he makes me angry. He cares more about changing the way things are than his own self-preservation, and I don't know if I can be with someone like that. Sometimes when I'm with him I feel like he's going to make everything I've ever worked for come crashing down. I know I can't be with him and I know he's the best thing that's ever happened to me."

Lying with Blake in his arms, a realization came to Paul that he found ironic considering his present situation: he had never known it before, but he did now, and it seemed so simple and clear. He loved David. He didn't know why it had been so hard to tell him, why it had been so hard to admit it to himself. How something so difficult and troubling, fun and joyous and silly, something that so filled him with fear and dismay could be called love, he didn't know, and yet there it was. He knew it now, and he wasn't sure if it changed anything, if it would make any difference in the tumultuous relationship, if it would save them or if it didn't matter at all.

They were quiet for a while. Then, Blake raised his head from Paul's chest, propping his face in his hand, his elbow pressing against the car seat below Paul's armpit.

"What's a Hollywood Reject?"

Paul laughed. "Where did you hear that?"

"In the bar Thursday night. Somebody called me that." He thought of the young blond boy in Capri pants who had leaned over the bar and alerted the bartender.

"It means you were spotted. They knew you were a cop." Paul explained the LAPD had taken to hiring strikingly handsome men—who had come to L.A. with dreams of making it in the movies, only to find themselves broke and jobless—to cruise bars and parks in order to entrap homosexuals into making a pass.

"I've never seen myself," Blake said grinning, "as a pretty boy."

"Oh," Paul said, "You look pretty pretty to me."

Blake kissed him, softer than he had before, but with firm, wanting lips. They stared at one another for a moment, then Blake slid on top of Paul, who could feel Blake beginning to give him the moves, full groin against full groin, slow and rhythmic at first like their kisses, then driving and compulsive.

"Maybe we shouldn't…" Paul breathed, but he didn't stop Blake as he unhooked their belts and slid down their trousers. They flipped off their shoes without untying them and dropped them on their jumbled clothes on the floor. Between deep kisses Paul licked Blake's face and there was salt on his cheeks from dried tears, licked his chest, his nipples and his armpits, the smell of them filling his senses.

Then, completely naked, Blake sidled up straddling him, his knees on the car seat on each side of Paul's chest. He tapped his hard cock insistently on Paul's chin.

"I want you to lather up my cock with your mouth, do you hear? Then I'm going to fuck you in the ass," he breathed huskily.

Paul licked at his bobbing cock, his hands gripping Blake's hairy buttocks, and once Paul captured his cock in his mouth, he could feel the gluteus muscles tighten and begin to thrust, forcing the cock deep in his throat. Looking down on him with a brutish expression on his face, Blake lifted Paul's head, gripping the nape of his neck with big hands, forcing his cock in deeper.

Blake raised his face toward the ceiling and let out a low moan. When he couldn't take it anymore he pulled out, and bent down and kissed Paul gently. And then, their eyes locked, he moved to the far side of the seat and spread Paul's legs. Paul could see the hard curve extending from Blake's groin, and all he wanted was to have that cock in him, he needed it, and nothing else in the world mattered. He cried out when Blake entered him.

Paul had never been with someone before who was so much stronger than he was. Blake must have had a good fifty pounds on him, and when Blake held him down Paul knew he didn't have the strength to fight him off if he wanted to, that Blake was completely in control of him, the bigger man's hands pinning his wrists, the weight of his body on top of him. For the first time he knew what it was like to be powerless under an assault.

He let out another little cry and then Blake covered Paul's lips with his mouth in a smothering kiss. Their eyes remained locked together and Paul could see something animalistic in the expression on Blake's face. The drive of his pelvis was hard and mean, as if this was the only thing that could push all the pain away.

Paul wrapped his legs around Blake's back, moving in rhythm with his thrusts. Blake's hand gripped Paul's dick, stroking hard, and all he wanted was to have Blake's come in him.

As Paul came, Blake shuddered on top of him, ramming his final thrust, his back arched, the muscles in his shoulders and arms tight, and he let out a howl.

Before they could take another breath, a bright flash of light that seemed to come from everywhere blinded them and the shock of the return to darkness sent scintillating crescents dancing across Paul's vision. He couldn't be sure, but he thought he heard the sound of a car engine outside speeding up the road.

Both men scrambled up, crowding together next to the window. They stared as the red taillights disappeared around a curve up the road. They watched, not uttering a word, long after the lights were gone and there was only darkness.

When he spoke, Blake's voice cracked.

"It was just the car's headlights, wasn't it? Flashing through the window?"

Paul stared at him. "It must have been," he whispered hollowly.

Suddenly they felt very naked and couldn't look at each other. They hurriedly began to put on their clothes.

After Blake got home that evening he took a long shower in the bathroom he shared with another resident of the rooming house who had gone out for the evening. First he had turned the water on and while he waited for it to get warm, the pipes clanking in complaint, he stood naked in front of the sink and evaluated himself in the mirror.

The blood was all gone, but his face was blotchy and a bit swollen, his lower lip thick. The skin on his cheeks was red and stung, but not from the beating in Beverly Hills. He ran his palms down his jaw line, knowing the irritation came from the abrasive rub of two men roughly kissing, stubble scratching against stubble, and he realized he had only felt another man's stubble on his cheek once before.

He felt confused and sore and exhausted and he wasn't sure who the man was whose face reflected back at him. Memories from that evening came to him in a jarring, sometimes violent, jumble of images. The sharp blow of the sap. His head swimming as he tried to rise from the sidewalk under the brutal assault. The cramped back seat surrounded by a world of night. Paul's gentleness as he washed away the blood on Blake's face, the softness of his tongue as he licked away dried tears. His own gut-wrenching admission of his final moments with Jack Spencer, opening a wound that never seemed to heal. And the swimming in his head as he held Paul down and pushed himself inside him, knowing that it was what he had to have, and that no amount of protest would have stopped him.

Afterward, they hadn't said much to each other as Blake had driven Paul back to the D.A.'s Office downtown, where Paul's car was parked. But they had both been thinking about the same thing. That light, that bright flash of light. He had a sick feeling inside him, that waiting feeling he had experienced before, the night they had taken Jack Spencer away.

He splashed cool water from the sink in his face, trying to wash away all the chaos in his head, and wondered grimly as he observed himself if it was too late to ice down his protruding lip, and if he could even find ice at this hour. He decided it wasn't worth the bother. He reached into the shower to test the water; lukewarm, but that was probably the best he was going to get. He stepped inside and pulled the curtain and found a hard bar of soap in the tray.

He wasn't able to get many suds out of the bar, and he ended up using it like a piece of pumice, rubbing it over his skin.

He thought about Paul as the stream poured down on his hair and face and ran in rivulets over his chest and back, thought about the man who had brought out so much emotion in him. Thought about Paul's body and how it had felt against his, the electric spark that ignited when Blake touched his skin. He had to remind himself he had only met the deputy district attorney two days before and hardly knew who he was. And he remembered the other guy, the one Paul told him about, the one he'd seen Paul kiss in the doorway. He had no idea where he stood in all of it, and that confused him even more. There was too much turmoil in his head to process and he didn't know what to make of any of it.

He hadn't noticed, but he had been scouring himself with the bar of soap so vigorously that the skin on his arms and legs and stomach were bright red and tingled in the spray cascading down on him.

The water ran cold before he finally turned the knob, leaving the nozzle to its incessant slow drip, and got out of the shower.

Across town Paul was showering, too, but for a different reason. He could smell Blake on him, on his skin, in his hair, and as he scrubbed himself with soap, loops of lather washing down his legs into the drain, once again he could feel Blake's big firm hands on him, caressing his body, pinning him down, holding him tight, gripping the nape of his neck. He stayed in the shower for a long while.

When he'd arrived home, David was just settling in on the living room couch after spending the afternoon at his synagogue and the evening having dinner at his parents' house. Seeing Paul come through the door, his tie in his hand, scuff-marked jacket over his shoulder, trousers torn at one knee, hair disheveled, David's eyes had opened wide. The book in his hands dropped into his lap and he began to rise.

"Oh, my God, what happened to you?"

"I'm okay," Paul had said, waving him off. "It looks worse than it is. I... got mugged downtown." He felt like a total cad lying to David, but he knew it wasn't the worst duplicity he had committed that night.

"Did you call the police?" David started across the carpet toward him.

Paul held up his hand to stop his progress. Suddenly he felt self-conscious, fearful that David would be able to smell another man on him. Afraid David could spot what he'd done by the way he walked. "It's all handled, David. I just really want to take a shower and forget the whole thing."

David stood looking at him curiously. "I'm just so shocked. You sure you're okay? Can I get you something?"

His lips were parched and he needed a drink, but he knew it wasn't from any robbery committed against him. "No, I'm fine." He went quickly into the bedroom, stripped off his clothes and jumped into the shower.

The intensity of his encounter with Blake stayed with him, sharp in every emotion, vivid in every detail, lacking in any regret, but that didn't stop him from feeling guilty and on some parallel track he felt fear that he had given into something, that there was no turning back, and everything was going to unravel. No matter how many times he tried to convince himself that no one would find out, he was haunted by their last moments in the back seat, and that flash of light that killed all intimacy between them.

When he got out and toweled himself off, he could still taste Blake in his mouth, the salt of his skin, the dried sweat of his armpits, and reached under the sink for a bottle of mouthwash and gargled.

"I had a long conversation with my parents this evening," David called to him from the bedroom through the ajar bathroom door.

"Oh, uh-huh," Paul called back, dabbing some cologne on his neck for reasons he'd be hard pressed to explain, "what about?"

David didn't answer and Paul figured this was a subject he wanted to discuss face to face. He opened the door and found David had gotten into bed, the lamp on the table providing illumination as he read his book. Paul felt oddly self-conscious again as he came across the room and climbed into bed.

"You feeling a little bit better?" David lowered his book and observed him sympathetically.

Paul nodded. He didn't want David to look at him, felt guilty seeing his compassionate expression, afraid that his own face would give him away. "You don't mind, do you, if we turn off the light? I just have a little headache. We don't have to go to sleep right away."

David reached over and switched off the lamp and the room went dark. He settled under the covers, then exclaimed, "Geeez, you smell like the perfume counter at The May Company."

"Oh, I'm sorry. I was just all hot and sweaty and I guess I went overboard."

"Well, you don't get attacked on the street every day. I just can't believe it. But, as you well know, I've never objected to having a hot sweaty man in my bed."

"You said you had a talk with your parents."

"Well, yeah. I've been thinking." He paused for a moment before continuing, as though he was putting building blocks together to form a sound foundation. "Maybe it wouldn't be such a bad idea for me to go to New York for that interview. I mean, I don't have to take the job if I don't want to. And it would be good for me, you know, like you said, to kind of mix with the movers and shakers in advertising."

Suddenly Paul felt gripped with sadness and wanted to put his arms around David and tell him not to go, but he didn't. He found himself holding his breath, as if his fate was to be decided in the next moment.

"It would be like a vacation kind of," David reasoned. "I could see the Statue of Liberty and all that stuff. I could stay a few extra days, get a hotel room in the Village, see the sights."

"I think that would be great," Paul managed to say. His voice sounded strange to him in the dark, and he wondered if David heard it too. Strained, as though his words caught in his throat. He was about to lose someone who mattered to him more than anybody else, and he knew all he had to do was ask David not to go and that would be the end of it. But lying there in the dark, he felt a spell had been cast over him, a magnetic pull he couldn't resist, and he knew with an aching heart that he wasn't going to do anything to save the relationship that mattered to him most.

◇◇◇

Late that night after Susan had gone to bed Dr. Socrates Stone sat reading a medical journal in his favorite recliner in the living room. Classical music played on the hi-fi. He had a hard time concentrating on the article's text, and his mind continued to drift to other things. On one hand, he had to admit, he was quite satisfied with himself for landing his new job with the LAPD. He was confident that—not right away, of course, but soon—he could think about putting a down payment on a house, perhaps in one of the developments springing up in the Valley. On the other hand, he had spent a restless Saturday afternoon worrying that none of his plans would come to anything, especially after the meeting he'd had with detectives on Friday, who seemed so resistant to his expertise.

Giving up on reading, Stone put his journal aside and went down the hall to check on Michael. He liked to do this every night, just go into his son's room after Susan had gone to bed and look at the boy as he slept. Leaning over the crib's bars, Stone pulled a blanket which had been kicked aside up to Michael's chin and tucked it in. He stood back, observing his child, and remembered something disturbing Susan had said when she'd come home from the playground that afternoon. She'd commented that Michael was one of those boys who didn't play with balls. He hadn't thought much about it when she'd said it, but as the day turned to evening, he couldn't seem to get it out of his mind. In the dimness of the room, lit only by a nightlight, he searched Michael's toy box, and when he didn't find what he wanted there, looked under the bed. He found a rubber ball, dusted it off, and placed it in the crib next to his son. Somehow, that made him feel better.

He heard the telephone ring and went swiftly into the living room and picked up the phone on the coffee table, wondering who could be calling at this hour, hoping it wasn't his mother with her weekly litany of complaints about his siblings or rehashed memories of her tribulations at the hands of his long deceased father. He just hoped Susan and Michael hadn't been awakened; once Michael woke at this hour, he'd fuss for the rest of the night, and Susan was hardly better, although the pills he had given her recently seemed to fix her bouts of insomnia.

Holding the receiver to his ear, he was surprised to hear the voice of a homicide officer he had met on Friday. He pictured the cop's florid face in his mind, and recalled that he had been one of the more vocal skeptics of the doctor's interrogation suggestions. As he listened to the cop's request, nodding to himself and occasionally responding with comments or questions, it dawned on him what an extraordinary opportunity was being presented, and adrenaline began to course through his veins.

"Yes, I think I can help you, Lieutenant Falk," he said when the detective had finished, hardly able to contain his excitement. "Is it possible for us to meet tomorrow morning?"

After he set down the phone, Dr. Stone felt a rush of anticipation and he realized his palms were wet. He had known it would happen, he just hadn't thought it would be so soon.

It was the case he had been waiting for.

Chapter 11

Paul woke that Sunday morning to the smell of David cooking bacon and eggs in the kitchen. He could hear sizzling and snapping from the skillet through the open bedroom doorway. The moment he opened his eyes a barrage of conflicting emotions from the night before came rushing back to him with sledgehammer force. He put pillows over his head to hide from the sunlight coming through the slats of the blinds and wished he didn't have to think. Not long after, the doorbell rang but he didn't respond, wanting only a few more minutes of oblivious sleep, even when he heard voices in the living room.

A moment later David stood in the bedroom doorway and said, "We have a guest."

Paul poked his head through the pillows. Behind David, Victoria Lynn was standing in the hallway. She looked tired and afraid. Even so, she was still strikingly beautiful, her simply combed blonde hair set off by her modest blue dress. She was holding a bulging purse with a thick stack of papers sticking out held together with a rubber band. She had two blue folders under her arm.

"You told me you would protect me," she said.

Sitting up in bed, an astounded look on his face, Paul said, "David, could you offer Miss Lynn some coffee? I'll be right out."

Once they were gone he got up and pulled on some slacks and was buttoning his shirt when David came back in.

"I hope it's okay to serve movie stars eggs over easy. Is that what they eat?"

"As long as you served it on my best China."

"I did. Along with the best silverware." His face turned sober. "What's going on?"

Paul hesitated, then gave David a run-down of what had happened since Charles Turner had been found hanging in his cell, while David commented, "Oh, that's why you asked about Pritchard Sondergaard," and "That's why you came to the *ONE* office wanting to know about Victoria Lynn." When Paul described the events of the night before, he ended the story with the assault in Beverly Hills. He needed to tell him the truth about what they were up against, that the authorities couldn't be trusted to protect them.

"I'm sorry, David. I didn't want you to worry. I shouldn't have lied to you about the mugging."

He felt like a total rat when David came over and hugged him.

"I just feel so bad," David said. "You look so banged up this morning."

They joined Victoria Lynn, who was eating her breakfast in the kitchen nook. The pile of documents sat on the table beside her plate, the purse gaping open on the floor. Paul sat next to her and David brought plates with eggs and bacon and toast for both of them.

Without make-up Victoria Lynn looked younger and more vulnerable than she had before, less a femme fatale and more a girl next door. But Paul knew neither of those extremes was a true picture of this woman, a farm girl from Washington State who had come to the city with nothing and had done what so many young women had to in order to succeed. He respected her and he felt sorry for her, because the dream she had sought had brought her nothing but unhappiness, and the difference between the real woman and the image she was forced to play could only bring despair.

"You said you could save me if you had those papers," she said.

"I didn't expect you to *steal* them." Paul flipped through the documents quickly as he ate, trying to find a smoking gun, but they were almost as incomprehensible as Mrs. O'Keife had described them. No doubt they were Department of Transportation documents, budgets, financial records. A private corporation was mentioned several times and he wondered what it meant. He looked through the blue folders, which detailed bank transactions, and bit his lip. He looked up and asked, "How did you get them?"

She tilted her head and looked at him with a sad expression on her face, and Paul knew she had compromised herself in a way no woman should ever have to with Mel Fischer in order to get access to the documents.

"Fischer," he said. "Does he know you took them?"

"He will when he wakes up. Although that could be quite a while, considering what I put in his drink."

"How did you get here?"

"I came in a cab. Why?"

"It can be traced. We've got to move. They'll be after you and the documents. I'll call the District Attorney's Office and get you into protective custody."

Victoria shook her head and held up her hands in a stop gesture that left no room for debate. "No. I'm getting out. I won't testify. I can't help you in your case. I don't know anything, except what I've already told you. You said if you had those papers you could bring all these people down. So do it. But do it without me. I'm going home."

"To Beverly Hills? You've got to be joking. You can't go to your house. They'll be watching. Victoria, they'll kill you now, do you understand? They'll kill you for what you've done."

"I mean home to eastern Washington. I need you to help me get out of L.A. without them knowing."

Paul knew from the tone of her voice he wasn't going to be able to convince her otherwise. And it could very well be the safest bet for her. The LAPD—at least Falk and Vincent—were involved in this conspiracy. Could he really promise her safety in protective custody? He looked over at David, whose eyes had been bouncing back and forth between them as they spoke like a ball on a tennis court. His eggs and bacon were getting cold on the plate untouched.

"David, what do you think?"

David shook his head at her ruefully. "You're not going anywhere looking like that."

Paul nodded in agreement. "You couldn't go to the grocery store without getting swamped by fans. How do you expect to secretly get out of the city?"

"If I can just change the way I look..." she began uncertainly.

"We've got to get you someplace you can hide and we've got to change your appearance before we can figure the best way to sneak you out of town."

Paul and David exchanged a glance and both said the same thing at the same time.

"Jeannie and Pat."

<><><>

That morning a patrolman on the beat had discovered Sergeant Hollings's abandoned Plymouth Savoy south of downtown in a run-down neighborhood on the lower edges of the University of Southern California campus near Vernon Avenue. Some of the larger houses had been made over into rooms for students, others showed the wear of homes owned by people too old and frail to keep them up. Negroes had begun to move into the fringes of the area.

Down the street the construction of the Harbor Freeway was making its arduous encroachment through one neighborhood after the next, mowing down houses and businesses in its wake, like a persistent root burrowing its way through unaccommodating soil, pressing on until it found water. Blake had read somewhere that when the expressway was finished it would reach all the way from downtown to the Pacific Ocean at San Pedro. Now it was a lot of concrete slabs, a chaos of wooden forms, and mountains of dirt, with mammoth trucks parked at all angles at the construction site. This morning it was quiet as a graveyard.

Detective Ryan had called him earlier and asked him to come by. Blake had an inkling his training officer was beginning to think that he might be the only one left in the department who could be trusted anymore. Especially after Hollings disappeared tailing Falk and Vincent when they'd slipped Peter O'Keife out of Lincoln Heights Jail.

As they stood in the street beside the car, Ryan looked him up and down. "You look like something the cat dragged in." His bushy eyebrows rose quizzically.

"Tough night," Blake said, without further explanation.

Ryan shrugged, observing Blake a moment, his hand resting on his firm beer belly, then he began to go down the list of what he'd discovered. "No sign of foul play. The doors were locked. No key in the ignition. I've already checked: there were no reports of anything going down in this neighborhood Thursday night."

Blake nodded. "It looks like he just parked here and left it." Blake could smell the booze on him and wondered if

165

his training officer had just come off an all-nighter at his favorite bar. At the moment he seemed sober enough.

"The question is, where did he go?"

"You've kept in contact with his wife. He never came home, right?"

"He disappeared without a trace." He was silent a moment. "I knocked on a few doors, but couldn't raise anybody. Maybe they're in church, or if they're students, maybe they're sleeping off last night's party."

The curtain fluttered in the front window of a sorry-shingled Craftsman style house across the street from where the Savoy was parked and Blake spotted a pale ghost of a face gazing at them. He nodded to Ryan and they took the cement walkway crossing a yellowing lawn to the sagging porch and knocked.

A wizened old man with a large nose and pendulous earlobes answered the door, peering at them through thick glasses with thick black plastic frames. They showed their badges but the old man waved them away without looking at them.

"'Bout time you people showed up. When it's not noise from the construction of the damn expressway during the day, it's the damn college kids and their parties on the weekends. We call the cops all the time but you people never come. We got niggers in the neighborhood now. And gunshots at night."

"You see who left that car?" Blake asked. "It was probably Thursday night."

"Let me go get my pad." The old man disappeared from the doorway and cooking odors drifted out from the dimness inside. He came back a minute later with a lined stationery pad in his hand scrawled with notes. "Let's see. Yes, the first car parked out in front on Thursday night at 9:23. Three men got out, two in the front first, then one in the back. The two escorted the third down the street."

166

Blake exchanged a glance with Ryan. Falk, Vincent and Peter O'Keife, he assumed.

"And then, at 9:27, another car—the one that's there now—rolled up. One man got out and went in the direction the others had gone."

"Did you see anything after that?"

He studied his notes. "At 10:35 the two men from the first car came back and got in the front seat and drove away."

"What about the others?"

"Never seen 'em again."

They didn't get any more from the old man, except generalized complaints about noise and Negroes, and they thanked him and returned to the street.

Ryan pulled his car keys from his pocket. "I'm going to drop by and see Hollings's wife. I don't think it's going to make her feel any better. But at least it's some news."

"I'll stick around. Knock on a few more doors. Check out the neighborhood."

"You won't find anything. I've already looked around."

When Ryan drove off, Blake started down the block. The houses looked tired and peaceful and lazy this morning, and no one stirred in any of the yards with their shaggy lawns or in any of the dark windows with their curtains half-drawn. He passed a service station on the corner and crossed the street.

A six foot plywood fence surrounded the construction area and it was harder to see inside up close than from across the way. Blake gripped the top of the fence and hoisted himself up, peering over. Beyond the concrete mixing trucks and makeshift tool sheds and piles of soil and gravel and sand, the gray pavement of the freeway snaked toward him from downtown in the distance, stopping abruptly in the foreground in a squalor of dirt being prepared for the pouring of concrete and half-built pylons with steel reinforcement cable jutting from their tops like straws.

He thought about what he was seeing for a long time.

Then he jumped to the ground and walked briskly across the street to the service station, found a dime in his pocket and went to a pay phone attached to a wall around the corner of the building. He dialed Paul Winters's home number. He had been a jumble of emotions he didn't understand since the night before, and he'd been putting off calling the deputy district attorney because he didn't know what he should say, how the two men were supposed to act towards each other. Were they supposed to pretend that nothing had happened the night before?

But it wasn't Paul who answered, and Blake realized it was the guy he'd seen him with. What was his name? Daniel? No, David. Hearing his voice, knowing he was at Paul's house on a Sunday morning, sent a mix of conflicting thoughts through his head that he didn't know how to decipher.

"He's not here right now. Can I take a message?"

Blake sensed tension in the voice on the phone, and wondered what it meant. He gave the cross streets of his location and asked for Paul to meet him here as soon as possible. He could tell David was writing it down.

"Um," David said. "It could be a while."

"Just tell him it's important. Tell him I've found something."

As he hung up the phone, Blake felt the presence of someone behind him, but before he could turn to let the person know he was done, he saw a blur in his peripheral vision, felt an explosion of pain and went out cold.

Jeannie and Pat lived in a bungalow on Genesee south of Sunset with a white picket fence crawling with rose bush vines. The yard had a severely green lawn and more plant life than any other house on the block; Paul knew that in a pinch Pat would dig up a bush or fledgling tree for a customer's landscaping and Jeannie would never notice the difference. Pat's red pickup truck, a somewhat shabby '46 Ford, sat in the driveway, its bed filled with buckets and shovels.

As Pat opened the door and she recognized Paul's companion standing on her porch, her eyes widened and her mouth gaped open, jaw hanging. "Did I just die and go to heaven?" She was wearing her obligatory jeans and a checkered shirt. She grinned bashfully at Victoria Lynn, quickly fluffing her unkempt straw-colored hair.

"Pat, this is Victoria. Victoria, this is Pat," Paul said by way of introduction. He quickly looked both ways down the street. "Can you let us in? I don't want anybody to see us." He had been worried a dark sedan was following them all the way from Brentwood until it turned off on Kings Road and he'd breathed a sigh of relief; even so, he knew it was only a matter of time before Fischer and his cronies would be hunting them down for the documents.

Pat brought them inside, a look of bemused curiosity on her face, and as Paul took off his hat and laid it on top of the stack of documents in his hands, she called down the hall, "Jeannie, sweetie, why don't you come here, honey?"

Jeannie appeared down the hall in the kitchen doorway with a dish towel in her hand. Her cotton-print house dress set off her auburn hair. Her head tilted quizzically as if she couldn't quite believe what she was seeing.

"Miss Lynn is in trouble," Paul explained. "And she needs your help. I have to be honest, there may be some danger involved."

Jeannie came down the hall and put her hand on Pat's forearm in a subtle show of proprietorship. The two women nodded to each other, as if coming to a silent agreement, and Jeannie said, "Of course, anything. First, can we offer you something, coffee, tea?"

"Tea would be fine," Victoria said. "Thank you so much."

"Same for me," Paul said.

"Miss Lynn, why don't you come in the living room where you'll be more comfortable?" Pat said, Cheshire grinning back at Paul and Jeannie as she took Lynn's arm and ushered her into the living room.

"Please, call me Victoria," Paul heard her say as she was taken away.

Paul followed Jeannie into the kitchen. She stopped abruptly once they were out of hearing range and folded her arms. "Paul, what's going on?"

"I need to help Victoria Lynn get out of town fast unrecognized. I want you to cut her hair and dye it brown. Make it short and dark. Can you do that?"

A light turned on in Jeannie's eyes. She grinned and went to a drawer, withdrew a pair of scissors and snipped it gleefully in the air. "With pleasure."

"This is serious, Jeannie. Her life may depend on it."

Jeannie nodded, her face going sober. "You know I'll do everything I can to help. Do you want to tell me what's going on?"

"The less you know the better. If you can just trust me. We'll be out of here in no time."

"Then dark hair it is. I'll go get my dyes. The kettle is on the stove, if you want to serve the tea."

"Short, but not butch," Paul warned. "Maybe give it some curls. Make her hair brown, mousy."

She nodded. "Can do."

"And not an ounce of make-up. And—do you have some old eyeglasses?"

"Uh, I have some pointy readers that were popular about five years ago."

"What about a dress?"

Jeannie pursed her lips and considered. "I'll find one that's a couple of years old… one that Pat refuses to wear."

"Perfect."

Jeannie went off to get her supplies and he put tea cups and the steaming kettle on one half of a serving tray, his pile of documents on the other, and went into the living room, where Pat was making sure Victoria Lynn had enough pillows behind her back to be comfortable on the couch.

Paul set the tray on a large oval coffee table. "Once we make sure nobody can recognize you, how do you want to get out of town?"

"The same way I came. You can just drop me at the train station. I have enough money on me to get home."

"All right. The sooner the better. Before they have anyone looking for you."

"There's one thing I have to do first."

Paul's eyes narrowed. "Okay, but it has to be fast. What do you need to do?"

"I need you to take me to Ruby's."

He shook his head. "Victoria, there isn't time—"

"I have to ask somebody something. Please, just do this for me."

The pleading tone in her voice stopped him from arguing with her.

"I'm ready!" Jeannie called from the kitchen, where she'd set a chair in the middle of the floor surrounded by newspapers.

Paul took the stack of documents from the tray and placed them on the coffee table and went to work. Pat paced back and forth in the living room with the nervous energy of a first-time father awaiting the birth of a child as she watched her idol transform back into a dowdy farm girl.

Although it would take an accountant to figure out exactly how they had gotten away with it, Paul began to see as he went through the documents what had set off warning bells for Peter O'Keife. The Department of Transportation project to build the expressway from downtown to San Pedro allocated tax money to a local construction firm owned by gangster Mel Fischer to perform the work. But money from Fischer's company was being siphoned off into a private corporation called Jones Development. The question was, what was being done with the money? He had an idea, and it made him sick. If he was right, it would connect the corruption at the agency responsible for constructing the super highways with the renewal project to raze Bunker Hill. It would connect all the players, the city council members who had voted to tear down a neighborhood, the lawyer who served them, the gangster on Sunset, and all the victims they had murdered along the way. Not all the documents appeared to be from the Department of Transportation, and Paul remembered Mrs. O'Keife had suspected her husband was following a trail of evidence.

Paul looked up from the papers spread on the coffee table. "Can I use your phone?" he asked.

Pat stopped pacing for a moment. "Sure, it's in the front hall."

Paul went into the entranceway and found the phone sitting on an inset shelf in a niche. He opened his wallet and pulled the card of Marvin Botwinick, the *Los Angeles Daily* reporter he'd met at the city council hearings, and dialed his number. After a few rings, Botwinick answered.

"This is Paul Winters, the deputy district attorney, we met Friday at the Bunker Hill hearings," he began. "Look, I'm sorry to be bothering you on a Sunday, but I was hoping you could help me."

"Hey," Botwinick said amiably, "I'm a big atheist Jew, you know, the kind the government is so afraid of, so you can call me anytime. Except May Day, that's my one holiday." Paul could almost see the reporter grinning as he raked his fingers through his thick beard.

"I was wondering if you might have any friends at the Hall of Records."

"Sure, what do you need? I can make a call on Monday and get you whatever information you want."

"I could do that myself. I need the information today. The sooner the better. Do you have any sources who can get into the building on a Sunday and look something up?"

There was a pause over the line, as Botwinick took a thoughtful puff on his pipe, then he said, "I think so. They can probably sneak me in, in fact. What do you want me to look up?"

"There's a corporation called Jones Development. I want to know if it has been buying up property in Bunker Hill."

"Now I'm interested. Give me an hour or so."

Victoria Lynn was escorted from the kitchen into the hallway flanked by Jeannie and Pat, who ushered her toward Paul as if the actress was being presented before royalty.

"Can you give me a second, Marvin?" Paul put his palm over the receiver. He smiled and shook his head. "I'd never know it was you."

The cool glamour girl was gone, replaced by a woman with a pretty face, a hairstyle that did nothing to set it off, and an ill-fitting dress Paul suspected was one of the garments Pat had been pressured to wear in years past on occasions when she was required to look femme.

"You can't know what a relief it will be for me to never see that dress again," Pat said, smiling.

Victoria pushed the eyeglasses down her nose and gazed at herself in the mirror on the wall. Her face fell for a moment, as if she recognized someone she had known a long time ago.

"I look terrible, don't I?"

There was a hint of a smile on her face and Paul couldn't help but feel she had said it with a certain sense of satisfaction.

"Not terrible at all," Paul said. "Just utterly unrecognizable."

"It's all washed away," Victoria said, nodding at Jeannie gratefully, "all the blonde. Gone like it was never there. I wish I could say the same for everything that's happened to me in this town."

"You're still beautiful," Pat gushed. "You'll always be beautiful. No one can take that away from you. And no one can take away how much you mean to so many young girls in the dark."

Victoria squeezed Pat's hand in thanks. "I'll remember that when I'm back home and I think about all the other stuff, when I try to tell myself it was all worth it."

Paul took his hand off the phone. "Marvin, you said an hour or so? You'll be able to reach me at a bar called Ruby's, over in West Adams. It should be in the book."

"Okay," Botwinick said, "but tell me, what is this all about? I mean, I smell a story. Is there something in this for me?"

"Yeah," Paul said, "if I'm right, probably the biggest story of your career."

◇◇◇

Ruby's was on the white lower middle-class cusp of West Adams, a wealthy colored neighborhood. The small one-story businesses on the block were shut tight this Sunday morning, the proprietors probably all in church, and the street was deserted. When Paul pulled up in front of the bar and he and Victoria Lynn got out, he didn't have to be told the heavy-set Negro woman with gray hair and a loose muumuu style print dress was Big Ruby. She was a legend in the community. She was wielding a mean hammer as she pounded a nail in a piece of plywood covering a front window. Standing beside her, his long bony arms holding up the sheet of wood, Paul recognized Alfred Washington from Pershing Square, still in his flowery garb, his burnt-red wavy hair now covered by a finely webbed net.

She tilted her head and smiled as they approached. "Miss Victoria, is that you?"

"Big Ruby," Victoria said, and her smile was genuine.

"I ain't never seen you in hair looking like that. They got you all made up for a part or something?"

"Something like that. Is Ruth here today?"

"My daughter's inside. We got the whole crew working here today."

Paul eyed the broken window she was covering with plywood. "What happened?"

She took him in from head to toe and Paul figured she was assessing exactly who he was and why a white man she didn't know was coming to her bar on a Sunday morning.

"The police don't like it when the whites and the colored come together, that I can tell you."

Paul addressed Alfred, who was still holding the board in place. "The charges against you have been dropped. You don't have to worry about that anymore."

"Thanks, but they'll just be back in another week or so to bother my pretty ass again."

"Not if you stay away from that park, they won't," Big Ruby scolded, landing the hammer on a final nail. As she stepped back to admire her work, and Alfred released his grip from the plywood, his sleeve caught on a nail and ripped.

"Oh, honey, I'm sorry," Big Ruby said. "When we're done here, I have some old clothes in a box in the back. There's a blouse you're gonna *love*."

Paul followed Victoria inside, and he wished he could say a wild Saturday night explained the destruction in the bar, but from what Big Ruby had intimated, he knew better. Tables and chairs were overturned, the mirror behind the bar smashed, bottles strewn on the floor. A group of people, both men and women, mostly colored but a few whites, were putting the place back together. Paul was surprised to see Jeff Dupuis in a corner trying to fix a table that had a broken leg. Behind the bar a pretty young Negro woman in her early twenties was sweeping up, and from the expression on her face when she saw Victoria come in, Paul knew she was the reason the actress had to come to Ruby's before leaving town. She put down her broom and proceeded around the bar. The two women came together and fell into each other's arms and kissed, deeply and passionately.

"Oh, baby, what did they do to your hair?" Ruth laughed and ran her fingers through the curls in Victoria's brown hair. "Where have you been? I've been reading the craziest stuff about you in the papers."

"I can't go into all that now. But I've got to talk to you. Is there someplace we can…"

Ruth indicated a door to the back office and she took Victoria's hand and led her there.

Jeff waved him over with a grin on his face. "Fancy meeting you here."

"I thought you were pulling double shifts since the quarter ended."

He blinked his eyes sleepily. "I am. But there was a police brawl here last night." His expression changed, and Paul remembered the Jeff he'd seen only once before, the one who was tired of waiting for the world to change, the one who carried the bitterness of the street. "Somebody called the cops and reported girl-girl and boy-boy dancing. I'm not sure if they mentioned it was blacks and whites. I guess the cops found that out when they raided the joint."

Paul nodded. Same sex dancing was illegal; some bars tried to protect customers by flashing a light or playing a particular song to warn dancers to stop when undercover vice cops arrived, but despite these defenses, arrests continued. The fact that the dancers were interracial was just gasoline on the flame.

"They came in with their nightsticks and broke the place up. We're here just trying to help Big Ruby out." His face changed back to the one Paul was familiar with at the jail as Jeff nodded and smiled at a white guy lugging a garbage can past them filled with broken glass toward the back door. The exchange between them told Paul that they were lovers. Big Ruby came inside with Alfred, the boarding over of the front window done, and they picked up boxes and carried them into a storage room. Paul glanced over at the office where Victoria and Ruth had disappeared. The door was halfway open, and he could hear their voices, but only snippets of their conversation. He heard Ruth cry, "Vic, I can't just up and leave!"

He turned to Jeff and asked, "So Ruth is Big Ruby's daughter?"

Jeff grinned. "We're *all* Big Ruby's kids. She never had any of her own, but she can't help herself. She picks up strays and they become her own. Ruth was on the streets when Big Ruby found her. That must have been, oh, about seven years ago."

"I see you got Alfred over here."

"I went by Pershing Square this morning and talked him into coming by, just for a visit. Did you know he was a dancer when he was a teenager? Traveled all over the country with a ballet troupe before the medical profession got their hands on him. I'm hoping he and Big Ruby will hit it off."

Paul grinned. He could see through the storage room doorway Big Ruby was going through a box of brightly colored blouses and offering those to Alfred that he liked. "I think they're getting along fine."

"Good. If we can build up some trust, maybe we can get him out of that park eventually."

A telephone on the wall by the restrooms began to ring, and Paul said, "You know, that could be for me." He answered it and found Marvin Botwinick on the line, puffing on his pipe.

"You were right, big swaths of Bunker Hill have been bought up by Jones Development."

Paul gripped the phone more tightly. "Recently?"

"Yeah, within the last several months."

"Tell me, who is the legal counsel for this corporation?"

"You mean, who is the lawyer handling it all?"

Paul could hear Botwinick flipping through pages.

"Oh," Botwinick said, "that's a familiar name."

"Let me guess," Paul said. "Pritchard Sondergaard."

"Okay, now it's time to tell me what's going on."

"Tax money that was supposed to be going to build the freeways was paid to a construction company owned by Mel Fischer, the gangster. He moved the money over to Jones Development, a front company designed to buy up Bunker Hill before the city council vote, then make a killing after the city council voted to acquire all the property and convert the area into a business and cultural center."

"Okay," Marvin said. "So Mel Fischer is behind it, with Pritchard Sondergaard running the legal side. He's known for having a lot of property downtown, buying more wouldn't raise suspicion. But that's not all, is it?"

"Every member of the city council who voted to gut Bunker Hill is in on the scheme. A massive rip-off at taxpayers' expense."

Marvin whistled. "They bought low and the city will pay high, all to be approved by the very city council who will profit from it."

"I can't be sure, but I think once they make their windfall profits on the Bunker Hill land, they'll just slip the original money they took back into the construction company. It will be like it was never embezzled in the first place."

"But the council members aren't listed on the board of directors of Jones Development. They were smart enough not to have their names tied to the company that would profit from their vote. How do you connect them?"

Paul thought of the blue folders he'd stashed in the trunk of the car along with the rest of the documents. "When Councilman Bullock was given the Department of Transportation documents by a whistleblower named Peter O'Keife, he did a little digging himself. I have a couple of folders that have banking statements showing transactions between Jones Development and each of the seven members of the council who voted to approve the Bunker Hill project." Paul went over the entire story with the reporter, starting with the death of Charles Turner and the disappearances—and undoubtedly the deaths—of Bullock, O'Keife and Hollings. O'Keife must have followed the trail of evidence all the way to the Bunker Hill scheme, because he'd undoubtedly approached Bullock because of his known opposition to the renewal project; the councilman was someone he could trust with the documents. Paul realized Bullock's homosexuality had nothing to do with his death; he'd been killed because he was going to use what he had discovered to expose the conspiracy and bring down the corrupt members of the council. He could hear Botwinick frantically jotting down notes. The only question Paul still couldn't answer was where the bodies had been buried.

When he was done, Marvin asked, "Paul, I don't want to look a gift horse in the mouth, but I've got to ask. Why aren't you going to the police with this? Why aren't you going to the D.A.?"

"I will. But I'm not sure which authorities I can trust anymore. The only thing that's going to keep this story from being buried in order to protect powerful people in this city is the public uproar when this is exposed."

"I need proof, concrete proof. I'll start writing the story, but this doesn't go to press until you give me the proof. My editor will insist on it. You have the documentation?"

"I've got it with me. I'll give you everything you need tonight. Just start writing."

"I'll call my editor and tell him to hold the front page."

After he hung up, Paul put a coin in the slot and called David, just to let him know how things were going. He felt a little guilty when David told him of Jim Blake's call. Just the thought of the two of them talking together, and David not knowing the truth, made him ashamed of himself. He took out a pad and pen from his pocket and wrote down the cross streets Blake had mentioned. Whatever was going on, whatever Blake had discovered, it would have to wait until Victoria Lynn was safely out of town.

Just as he hung up the phone, Victoria Lynn came out of the back office, alone, a tear on her cheek, a devastated expression on her face, and walked to the front door without saying a word. Paul followed her outside and opened the passenger door for her and she got into the car. When he slid behind the wheel, he touched her gently on the arm and said, "I'm sorry."

"That's okay," she said lifelessly. She looked out the window. "I came to Hollywood with nothing, and I leave with nothing."

There didn't seem to be anything left to say as he drove her to the train station.

Chapter 12

Blake woke with a terrible pounding in his head. It took him a moment to realize he was lying naked on a cement slab in a jail cell.

Something was hanging directly above his head from a pipe in the ceiling. At first it didn't register in his mind what it was, and then, once it did, he sat bolt upright. It was a belt, and he knew without seeing it before that it was the belt Charles Turner had been hung with.

As he jumped up from the slab his head swam and his legs faltered but he made it to the door.

"Help!" he shouted. He banged on the heavy metal door, but nobody came. The door had a small peephole but he couldn't see anything through it except a cement block wall on the other side of the corridor. He pounded his fist on the door until it hurt, but nobody responded.

Exhausted, he turned and leaned against the door, trying to catch his breath, taking in all the details of the cell. He couldn't be sure where he was, other than that he was in jail, but something told him just to make a point they had put him in the cell Charles Turner had died in.

The interrogation room was stuffy and claustrophobic: a wobbly table and three hard wooden chairs, with a one-way mirror in the wall. The light hanging on a cord from the ceiling had a metal shade like a funnel, but that didn't make the bulb any less naked. It shined harshly on the white glossy walls and Blake squinted in the glare. His head still ached as he sat alone in the room, but his body seemed strangely numb to him, as if an electrical circuit connecting the two had been switched off. His tongue was dry and felt two sizes too big. At least they had given him his clothes back.

He had been there a long while when the door opened.

A tall thin man wearing a conservative suit who appeared to be in his early thirties stepped inside and closed the door behind him. He didn't have the look or the world-weary demeanor of a detective, and this unexpected circumstance made Blake far more wary than if a couple of rough cops had entered to give him a beating before questioning. The man looked like an intellectual. He adjusted his glasses on his nose, observed Blake a moment, and unbuttoned his suit jacket. He was holding a file in his hand.

"My, it's warm in here, isn't it?" the man said pleasantly.

He sat down in the chair across from Blake, who didn't answer, but waited for the man to continue.

"My name is Dr. Stone, Dr. Socrates Stone. I've been asked to consult on this case."

"Somebody hit me on the head," Blake began. He was surprised that his voice came out sounding plaintive rather than angry. Maybe it was the way his tongue was sticking to the roof of his mouth. "Then they threw me into a cell in solitary—"

"That's not why I'm here."

"You know I'm a cop, right? You know I'm LAPD?"

"I know who you are."

Dr. Stone took the file, which had rested on his lap, and laid it on the table. "I want to help you. You understand that, don't you, Jim? I'm a psychiatrist employed by the police department, but what I want, more than anything else, is to help you. Do you believe that, Jim?"

Blake didn't move for a moment, and then slowly he nodded his head.

Stone opened the file and began to study the report inside, slowly turning the pages, his head almost imperceptibly shaking.

"It's a shame. You could have such an extraordinary career in law enforcement."

Blake leaned forward, his hands gripping the table. "I haven't done anything—"

The psychiatrist held up his hand. "Please. We know that isn't true." His hazel eyes met Blake's and held. "You know it and I know it." He closed the file and placed his hand on top of it. "I've looked at your record. Both your military service—and other than lying about your age," and here Stone smiled at him indulgently, even fondly, "which, I think, we can pass off to youthful exuberance, and is more a merit considering the circumstances than a defect—and your years of service as a police officer in Wisconsin, are exemplary."

A kernel of optimism began to grow in his mind, and for a moment Blake had hope that everything could be straightened out.

"Yes," Blake said. "I was investigating a case, and I had just made a call at a phone booth, and all of a sudden—"

"There are a couple of officers who want to talk to you," Stone said, cutting him off.

Blake threw up his hands in the air. "Look, doctor, I don't even know what I'm doing here."

Stone observed him but didn't answer. He rose and went to the door, taking the file with him, hesitating a moment with his hand on the knob. He looked back and Blake couldn't read the expression on his face when he said, "You understand that anal sodomy carries a lifetime prison sentence."

And then the doctor was gone, the door closing behind him.

Something fundamental inside Blake was crushed when he heard those words and he knew his life would never be the same. The nightmare he had feared, the nightmare that was real, the flash of a light searing the darkness in the car last night, came back to haunt him, and a voice in his gut that he didn't want to believe told him it was over, that nothing could save him.

He knew he had to concentrate and be at the top of his game for the interrogation to come, that his future depended on it, but he couldn't no matter how hard he tried. As he waited, his mind raced in circles but always came back to the same place. They had something on him but he didn't know how to react until he knew the extent of their evidence. If it was bad, it would be really bad. There would be no defense and there would be no way out.

He began to sweat. It had been hot in the room all along, but now he felt beads of moisture on his brow. He got up and began to pace. He wasn't hungry but his stomach felt hollow and ached. He hadn't had anything to eat since breakfast, and that was just coffee and a roll. Where were these cops who wanted to talk to him? How long were they going to keep him here? How many hours had he been in custody? He wasn't sure anymore if it was night or day.

It had been morning when he'd been knocked unconscious but that seemed a long time ago. How long had he been in the cell? Three hours? Five? Seven? He felt disoriented, unsteady, like he was walking on a rocking boat. As he passed the mirror, he thought he saw shadows of movement behind, and he self-consciously wiped his brow with his sleeve and sat back down in the chair, as if pacing was an admission of guilt.

It seemed like an hour before the door opened again and two officers came inside. Blake's eyes narrowed when he didn't recognize either man. He had thought for sure the officers Dr. Stone had told him were coming would be Falk and Vincent and he would be able to confront them, expose their activities to whoever was behind the mirrored glass. Now he just felt confused.

What did they want from him?

The older cop had a blond crew cut, a stocky figure, deep horizontal crevasses in his forehead that put him in his forties, and a swagger that pegged him for once being a military man. The other wasn't much older than Blake, a slighter man with a sympathetic young face and gentle brown eyes. Both wore flashy ties with somber suits.

As they sat in the two chairs across from Blake, the older one said, "I'm Detective Reitman, this is Detective Mandel. We want to ask you a few questions."

Blake was both wary and relieved. Maybe he could be out of here soon. A few questions. How long could that take?

"Okay." He tried to swallow but there was no saliva in his mouth. "Look, can I have something to drink?"

Mandel began to rise, but his partner put his hand on the younger man's arm, signaling him to sit back down. "You can have something to drink later," Reitman said. "We just have a few questions." Mandel shrugged and gave Blake an empathetic look.

"So, Jim," Reitman began, "What were you doing in that car last night?"

Blake's heart sank. So they knew. They knew everything. But knowing and proving were two different things. He could still walk out that door. They hadn't brought anything with them, and that could only mean they had no hard evidence. He could beat this. He had before.

"Nothing."

Reitman leaned back in his chair and folded his arms. "C'mon, you can do better than that. I've been a cop for ten years. I know what queers do in the back seat of a car."

The word jarred him in a way he hadn't expected, to be called a queer, to be put in that category, and he was afraid to look down at his hands on the table because he could feel them beginning to shake.

"I don't know what you're talking about."

"Why are you protecting him?"

"I'm not protecting anybody."

"Then tell us his name."

Blake remained silent, knotting the fingers of his hands together to stop the shaking.

"We already know who he is, Jim. We followed the two of you to where you parked the car. We just need you to show you're willing to play ball with us."

"If you already know who it is—"

"Play ball with us, Jim. Show we can count on you to be honest."

Mandel, who hadn't said a word, leaned forward. There was no contempt in his voice, only kindness, as if he just wanted to understand. "Are you in love with him?" he asked quietly.

The question struck him almost as hard as the slur uttered by the young cop's partner.

"No." Blake's lips were parched, bloated, burning. "I'm not in love with anybody."

There was a knock at the door, and Mandel got up to answer it. He conferred for a moment with someone Blake couldn't see, then looked back into the interrogation room, giving Blake a sympathetic nod, then went out the door and shut it behind him.

Reitman snapped his fingers to get Blake's attention. "You seem easily distracted, Jim. What are you staring at? Would you prefer my young colleague continue your questioning?"

"You promised me some water."

"All in good time."

They didn't speak for a long while and Blake began to wonder if Reitman was waiting for his partner to return before continuing the interrogation. As time went on he began to notice Reitman looking at him with a strange assessing gaze. The detective tilted his head, as if something had just occurred to him, and a smile, subtle as a baby's breath, played on his lips.

"Do you find me attractive?"

Blake stared at him incredulously. At first he wasn't sure he'd heard him correctly.

"Do you want to suck my dick, Jim?"

In confusion Blake glanced over his shoulder at the mirror, as if appealing for witnesses, then back at his interrogator.

"Nobody's there. We're all alone. Just you and me. So, do you want to suck my dick, Jim?" He pushed his chair back, legs spread wide. He rested his hands on his thighs. "Come on. No one will know. Is that who you are, Jim? One of those guys who sucks other guys' cocks? Is that what you want for your life?"

Blake stared at his hands clasped together on the table and shook his head.

"I didn't think so," Reitman said.

There was a gentle rap at the door, then Mandel stepped inside with a tall glass of water. He smiled at Blake.

"I remembered you said you wanted some water."

He placed the glass on the table in front of Blake. Looking annoyed, Reitman pushed back his chair, got up and sauntered to the door. "I'm going to take a break. It's getting hot in here." He glanced back at Blake and Mandel. "I'll leave you two alone." The door shut behind him.

Mandel sat and watched Blake drink, long slow gulps that never seemed to quite quench his thirst. He drained the glass and wanted more.

Grimacing, Mandel said, "I'm going to be honest with you. Interviewing another cop, this is all new to me. I just made detective last week. I hope Detective Reitman isn't being too tough on you. There's something I want you to know, Jim. No matter what you did last night you and I are still on the same team. We're cops. We stick together through thick and thin. Our lives depend on it. Look, I'd rather give a break to a cop than a lawyer in an expensive suit any day, but I can't help you if you don't help me."

At first Blake couldn't fathom what the young cop was getting at, and just stared. A lawyer in an expensive suit? And then, with a growing sense of unease, he began to surmise whom he was talking about. And he began to wonder if he was the only one being interrogated.

Reitman poked his head in the doorway and said, "I hate to break up this love nest, Mandel, but you're needed in interrogation room three."

Mandel nodded at Blake before he got up. "Think about what I said." He went with Reitman and the door closed again.

It seemed like an hour passed. Blake's bladder was full and he really had to go. His back ached, sitting in that hard little chair, and he kept shifting in the seat to try to make himself more comfortable. He couldn't stop thinking about what Mandel had said. He'd rather give a cop a break than a lawyer. What had he meant? What was going on in interrogation room three?

He got up and began to pace. What was taking them so long? He went over and tried the door. It was locked. He pounded on it.

"Hey," he shouted, "I need to use the restroom!"

He looked at the mirrored glass. "I need to use the can!" Was he just imagining it, or were shadows shifting behind the glass? He waited, but nobody came. He kept thinking about what Mandel had said. He knew that detectives didn't interrogate suspects in two different cases at once. When more than one detainee was interrogated, it was because they both were involved in the same crime. It was to play one suspect off against the other. To see who would turn on the other first.

He slammed on the door again. "C'mon, you bastards!"

Pacing across the room, he turned to find Reitman coming through the doorway, closing it behind him. He was carrying a leather briefcase with shiny brass locks.

"I need to use the bathroom."

"I can bring you to the restroom in a few minutes."

"No, I want to go now."

"Jim, I think you'll want to look at this."

Reitman sat at the table and laid the briefcase on it without waiting for Blake's response. He flipped the locks on each side of the handle.

Then Blake realized what the briefcase meant. Before he had been relieved they had no physical evidence, had taken strength and hope from it. Now he knew his life rested upon what was in that case. Slowly he sat down.

Opening the briefcase, Reitman took a nine by eleven manila envelope out. He closed the case, then placed the envelope on the table in front of Blake. Blake's eyes rose from the envelope to the interrogator.

"Want to see what's in it?"

Blake just stared at him without saying a word.

"Go on." Reitman indicated the envelope with a dismissive wave of his hand. "Open it."

A terrible knot began to coil and tighten in his stomach as Blake reached over and held the envelope in his hands.

"Go ahead."

A crushing weight of despair rested on his shoulders and he knew what he would find inside. If he could have died right then—not continued a moment forward—he would have. His mouth was dry again and he licked his lips as he opened the envelope and pulled out the contents.

It was a black and white photograph, the lighting harsh and stark as a porn reel, of two naked men in the back seat of a car, one on top of the other, the man on the bottom's legs in the air. There was no doubt what one man was doing to the other. Though Blake was photographed from the back, he could see his own head was turned slightly, as if in the final second he had become aware of the photographer's presence behind him. That one movement had sealed his fate and made him unquestionably identifiable. It seemed unreal, unfair, because as he racked his brain he couldn't remember a moment of warning before the camera had flashed silver light through the window. His head obscured the face of the man on the bottom, protected him from the flash's glare. Only the side of Paul's head, his ear, his jaw, was exposed.

The photo had caught him in his final thrust. The man on the bottom's legs were wrapped around his torso, clinging to him, forcing his cock inside him harder, and Blake remembered how wonderful that had felt then and how sick and filled with horror it made him now.

His face burned and he couldn't look up from the photograph. He felt heat and shame and disgust that didn't seem to be his at first, but imposed on him in this stuffy little room with eyes watching behind glass, eyes everywhere, and revulsion spread through him sour and poisonous as if he'd been forced to swallow arsenic.

"Tell us his name, Jim."

Dully he told himself they already knew. They had to know. Who else could be in interrogation room three? He heard himself say, "I want a lawyer."

"That's all you have to say?"

"Get me a lawyer."

"No lawyer would take this case. But I'll tell you what I can do for you." Reitman picked up the briefcase and slammed it against Blake's head with such force that Blake was thrown off his chair. He landed hard on his back on the floor, the chair clattering down beside him. Before he could take in a breath Reitman was on top of him pummeling his face with his fists. "You make me fucking sick," Reitman screamed. "You sickening queer."

Blake tried to ward off the blows, but he was so dizzy he could hardly tell where they were coming from. When he felt like he was about to pass out, he became aware that someone was pulling Reitman off him and the barrage of fists ended. Then he heard Dr. Stone scolding the detective and pushing him out of the room. As he tried to get up, righting the chair and climbing onto it, Blake saw that he had wet his pants, and a long dark stain pooled in his groin and ran down his leg. The cuff of his pant leg dripped. He could smell urine.

Dr. Stone took the chair across from him and shook his head. "I'm sorry, that was totally unprofessional of him. But you have to understand his anger. You've shamed them all, you've shamed every cop in the LAPD in the worst way an officer can. You've offended the manhood of every policeman on the force. No wonder they're angry."

Stone observed him a moment before he continued. "I want you to know I'm not like them, Jim. They're cops. Their job is to arrest and to judge. But that's not who I am. They see a criminal, Jim, a criminal who has debased their profession in the most revolting way imaginable. But I'm not a cop. I'm a psychiatrist. And that's not how I see you,

Jim. That's not how I see you at all. I see a troubled man, a man who needs my help."

His eyes shining like coals, Dr. Stone's face became earnest. "But don't get me wrong. Don't think I'm a pushover for perverted behavior. For God's sake, Jim, you're a cop. You know the sickening things those people do. In parks. In bathroom stalls. To any young man on the street they can get their hands on. And when a young man can't be found, children, young boys. You know it's true. You're not like that. I can tell just by looking at you. You're not one of them. You never were. You never could be. You're just confused. These people mix you up, make you think you're something you aren't. It's to their advantage to do so. And once they have you, a guy like you, a man, a real man like you, once they get their claws in you, they'll never let go."

The psychiatrist stared at him a long while, nodding his head appraisingly. "Do you want my help, Jim? Would you like me to help you?"

Blake didn't know what he meant. His jaw hurt so badly from being struck by the briefcase he was afraid it was broken, and there was ringing in his left ear. He wasn't sure, but he thought he heard his voice croak, "Yes."

"First I want you to put that filthy thing away."

At first Blake didn't understand, and then he realized the photo lay in front of him on the table. He took it and slid it back into the envelope. Stone picked the briefcase off the floor and put the envelope inside.

"It can be as simple as that, Jim. It can all go away."

"I don't understand."

"You have a choice, Jim. Are you going to save your career, or are you going to throw it all away? You're a good man, I know you are. But good men can make mistakes. Ten minutes in the back of a car doesn't have to define your life. It's not who you are. It doesn't have to be. I want you to ask yourself, why are you protecting someone you don't even know? Why are you throwing away your freedom for someone who feels absolutely no loyalty to you at all?" Stone glanced over his shoulder at the door behind him. "And I can tell you, and I know this for a fact, he doesn't care a whit about you. These people will betray you, they always do. They're cowards, Jim. Every one of them. They wouldn't do what they do if they weren't. They'd kill themselves if they weren't."

There was a knock at the door, and Stone got up and opened it. The doctor held the door partially shut, and Blake couldn't see who he was conferring with, only that the conversation was animated, and Stone kept looking back at him with an expression of consternation on his face. Finally he addressed Blake by saying, "Excuse me, something has come up." He frowned at Blake as he left the room. "Think about what I said."

In the observation room, Dr. Stone had a conference with Lieutenant Falk and Detective Vincent and the two other officers who had been called in on the case under the doctor's advice. He was thrilled with how he had impressed the detectives but didn't want to show just how pleased he was with himself. He didn't know what the bigger picture was, and he didn't have to know. All he needed to do was give the detectives exactly what they wanted. He could tell already that he would have a long association with them and they would spread the word of what he had done here today. He glanced through the glass into the interrogation room, where Blake was hunched over the table, his face in his hands.

"We're exactly where we want to be," Stone said. He nodded to Reitman and Mandel. "You've played your parts very well." He flipped through the pages of his file. He hadn't done so badly himself. His mention of betrayal, he thought, was especially clever, considering what he had read in Jim Blake's military file. He had set up all the pieces beautifully.

He turned to Mandel. "It's your turn. You know what to say."

Mandel came into the interrogation room looking visibly distraught. He was carrying a document and a pen. He shut the door behind him and stopped to gaze angrily at Blake. "You'd better come clean with me right now and tell me the truth," he said in a seething voice. All the sympathy in his face was gone, and all that was left was boiling rage. His demeanor was so changed that Blake knew something had happened. "I trusted you and I stood up for you and now I hear the truth about what happened in that car."

Blake sat up at attention. He was sure now he had been right. Paul Winters had been arrested too. He was in the next room. That's what all the commotion had been about, all the going back and forth between interrogation rooms. They were waiting to see who would turn on the other first. But what was Mandel talking about? What had Paul told them?

"Tell me right now," Mandel demanded. "Did you trick that guy into getting in that back seat with you?"

Suddenly Blake could see where this was going and he understood the fury on his interrogator's face. The room tilted and his stomach seemed to float in the air and for a moment he thought he was going to throw up.

Mandel stared at him, his jaw slowly dropping open. "It's true, isn't it?" he said, in almost a whisper. "You got him to get into the back seat with you and then you committed forcible sodomy upon him."

"No!" Blake shouted. "That's not what happened. Is that what he said?"

The walls seemed to close in on him. For the first time the realization of how compromised he was seared him like a blowtorch. He had been on top of the other man and there was no doubt of his culpability. But the man on bottom could claim otherwise. Then something else dawned on him. As an attorney, Paul would know all the ins and outs of how the game was played, how to turn a felony charge against him into a misdemeanor or even a get-out-of-jail-free card. How to save himself. And Paul had friends, so many friends, in the D.A.'s Office, in high places. Of all people, a prosecutor would know there was no way they were going to let both of them walk. Somebody had to take the fall. Bitterly he thought what a dirty trick it was that only his face was identifiable. That he was the one left on the hook. He wondered, in that final moment before the flash of light, if Paul had seen the camera looming in the window and instead of crying out a warning just turned his face away to save himself.

"That's what he's saying, Jim. You fooled him into getting into that back seat with you and then forced yourself on him."

"That's a lie!" As soon as he said it, he wondered if it was true. Had he forced himself on Paul? If it had been a woman and he had done that, held her down, fucked her like that, unable to stop himself, it would have been rape, wouldn't it?

Mandel shook his head, crossing his arms at his chest. "If that's the case, all bets are off. I can't save you. I wouldn't want to. You're going to spend the rest of your life in prison, Jim, and it's going to be hard time. Do you know what hard time does to a man?"

"It's not true," Blake said. "It's not true."

Mandel came quickly to the table and sat across from him. His eyes were sympathetic again, pleading. "Jim, you need to make a deal while you still can. It's you or him."

He slid the document halfway across the table and placed the pen on top of it.

Blake couldn't think anymore. He just wanted to shut his eyes and die. He sucked on his swollen lip, and a memory came to him that seemed like a long time ago but was from just the night before. He could almost feel Paul gently taking the hard lump in his mouth, his tongue caressing, and how sweet it had been. Blake felt a tear run down his cheek.

"Just give us a name." Mandel glanced back at the door as if he expected a knock any moment. "Jim, I'm going to be frank with you, there isn't much time." He pushed the paper across the table closer to Blake. "If you sign this, we can make this whole thing go away. Just sign it, and give us a name. Just to show you can play ball. A name, Jim. Just a name."

Jim Blake rested his face in his hands for a long while before he spoke. For the first time in over a decade of uncertainty he understood what Jack Spencer had felt that night alone in a claustrophobic room and what it took to break him down.

Chapter 13

David was sitting at the dining room table when Paul returned home.

He had dropped Victoria Lynn off at the train station downtown in order for her to catch the evening train to Spokane, then, mindful he had to protect the documents locked in his trunk, dropped by his office and placed them in his safe. He'd keep them there until his appointment with Marvin Botwinick later in the evening. Before stowing them away, he'd spent several hours tagging the documents he felt were most important to proving the conspiracy, the ones Botwinick would need to convince his editor to run the story, and had written up a detailed account of the case as it unfolded over the last week and a half.

Even though he'd called Jim Blake both at home and at the LAPD, he couldn't track him down. On his way from the train station he had driven by the cross streets Blake had left in his message, but Paul couldn't figure out their significance. There was a gas station on the corner of a block of run-down houses across from the freeway construction site. He couldn't understand what Blake had discovered or why he'd disappeared. The sun had gone down by the time he headed back to Brentwood.

When David had no reaction to him coming in the door—he just sat there staring down at the table—Paul knew something was wrong.

"David," he said softly, "what is it?"

As he came into the dining room, he saw a manila envelope sitting on the table in front of David, and a knot tightened in his stomach. There was no address on the envelope, which suggested to him that somebody had left it at the front door, and even though his name was scrawled across it in ink, he could see that David had torn the envelope open.

He knew what it was without even looking inside. He had known this was coming since that flash of light the night before, no matter how much he had tried to push it to the back of his mind and to convince himself otherwise.

"Oh, David," he said. "I'm so sorry."

David didn't look at him. He just kept staring at the envelope in front of him. Paul could tell he'd been crying from his flushed cheeks. When David finally spoke he seemed far away.

"I know it's you. Other people won't be able to tell, I don't think." Now he looked up at Paul, his eyes welling. "But I know."

He could hardly take the look of hurt and dis-appointment in David's eyes. Feeling sick to his stomach, Paul picked up the envelope and slid the picture out. As soon as he saw it, he knew the life he had known in the last thirty years was over, that his memories would be forever split between the world before and the one after. He knew he wouldn't be able to survive this, that his career was finished, that colleagues at the District Attorney's Office would abandon him, that he would be disbarred. Everything he had worked for was lost.

David's voice came out like a croak. "What do you think they want?"

"I don't know." It could be simple blackmail, simple dirty blackmail with no connection whatsoever with the case he had been investigating, but he doubted it. More likely, Falk and Vincent must have followed them after the assault in Beverly Hills, waiting and watching in the dark. If that was the case, he still wasn't sure what they wanted. To drop his investigation as Mel Fischer had demanded the night before? Was the picture a bargaining chip to force him to return the Department of Transportation documents Victoria Lynn had stolen? It must be. And if he gave in to them, would their threat go away? Would they give him the picture negative in exchange for giving them what they wanted?

Or was this just the beginning? A far worse fate occurred to him than giving them the documents in return for the negative. What if he did as they commanded, and then they held on to the evidence against him? What if their goal was not to expose him, but to sit back and wait, watching him from afar as he climbed the ladder that so many expected him to in the next few years, culminating in his election as the District Attorney of Los Angeles. Yes, that would be far more beneficial to them, to hold the negative of the photo in perpetuity in a safe somewhere, ready to be taken out whenever he made a move to their detriment. They could control every decision he made regarding which crimes to prosecute and which mobsters to target for prosecution. In fact, it would be in their interest to help him along the way, not just in the District Attorney's Office, but beyond. And always he would be at the beck and call of the shadowy forces that held the photograph.

Paul sat down hard on the chair next to David as if someone had struck him in the abdomen with a sledge-hammer.

"There's a telephone number on the back," David said dully.

Paul turned it over and looked at the exchange for a moment. He couldn't tell, but he wondered if it was an office number for The Swallow Inn. He studied the photograph again, and once the hard slap of recognition and shame had passed, Paul realized that David might be right, and a ray of hope gave him strength. Only the side of his face was revealed, hardly enough to prove anything. He knew the mere accusation could destroy him, but he was a lawyer, and in a court of law this wouldn't stand. He could fight it. The same wasn't true for Blake, who was easily identifiable, and with far more concern than before Paul wondered why he hadn't been able to get in contact with him all afternoon.

Paul rose from his chair, feeling a little more in control of the situation, and went to the telephone table beside the front door.

David turned in his chair. "If they want to bargain for the Department of Transportation documents, you can't do it. You can't give in to them."

Paul didn't answer; he dialed the number. He had no idea who was going to pick up, but he wasn't surprised when he heard the voice of Pritchard Sondergaard. He pictured him in one of Mel Fischer's upstairs offices.

"I got your message," Paul said quietly.

"Good. You're going to give us the girl, and you're going to give us what she stole from us."

At least he knew now what they wanted. "The girl is gone. She's out of it. That's not negotiable."

"You're not in any position to make demands, my friend. You will bring her to us and you will bring what she took."

"I just told you," Paul said stiffly, "she's out of it. Forget her. She knows nothing and she can't hurt any of you. She's not what you want, and you know it."

"You don't seem to understand it's not up to me."

"Then tell your masters I won't play ball."

Sondergaard's voice went from haughty to seething in record time. "You are a foolish little man and I'm not going to die because of your little games. Do you realize who you're dealing with here? These people will kill us all, do you understand? They'll kill us all and they won't think twice about it."

For the first time Paul realized that Pritchard Sondergaard was scared, too. That anyone in this organization was expendable, even the high-profile lawyer who had brokered the land deal, who had probably brought all the parties in the conspiracy together. A gangster like Mel Fischer wouldn't care how much Sondergaard had done for him; he'd only remember that the lawyer had brought Victoria Lynn into his place of business and she had had the audacity to humiliate him in the bedroom by drugging him and stealing from him.

"If you delay, that photograph will be distributed to the press, the police and your boss. Is that what you want?"

"You can't tell who that is in the picture," Paul said. "You have nothing."

There was a pause, and Paul could almost hear Sondergaard smile. "We have a sworn confession from the other party involved in the crime that that's you in the picture. And since he's a police officer, I think he'll be believed."

Paul put his head in his hand, still gripping the phone to his ear, and knew it was over. He didn't doubt what Sondergaard had told him for an instant. They had won. He knew now why Jim Blake hadn't answered any of his calls and a feeling of utter despair descended over him. Even now, barely able to stand on his own two feet, hunched over, clutching the phone, he could still remember the warmth of Blake's body against his and something died inside him.

"Paul, are you there?"

He could hardly speak. "I'm still here."

"I think we can come to terms, don't you? Mutually beneficial terms?"

"The negatives for the documents. I can't offer you anything more," he heard himself say.

"I think that would be a satisfactory arrangement. I think I can convince my clients that the girl means nothing. Bring the documents here to The Swallow Inn within the hour. I'll tell Fischer's men to bring you up to the office."

"I can't. I don't have them with me. I'll have to go get them. Say, two hours."

There was silence over the line. "You're not planning to break our agreement, are you?"

"No," Paul assured him, with no energy left to fight, "I'll be there in two hours."

Sondergaard hesitated before hanging up, as if he wasn't entirely convinced and was pondering other options, and then the phone went dead. When Paul put down the receiver David stared at him from the dining room table, rising to his feet.

"You can't do it, Paul."

Paul went to the living room couch and sat down. Every bone and muscle in his body seemed to ache. He put his face in his hands, his elbows resting on his knees. "They have a sworn statement saying that was me in the picture."

David came slowly toward him. "I don't care. Are you listening to me? You can't give in to them."

Paul looked up at him. "What other option do I have?"

"You've got to fight them!"

"David, don't you understand what this means? If I don't do exactly what they say and they expose me, it's prison. I know what happens in cases like this. They'll use me as an example that people in authority can't get away with this any more than the common guy. They'll throw the book at me. It means losing everything. Do you understand? And it won't just be me. It will touch every-body we know. All our friends. Everybody will be tainted by association."

He thought about what had happened in Boise, Idaho, just the year before, when a few politically motivated accusations of homosexual activity with teenagers had burgeoned into state-wide hysteria fanned by the press that led to the interrogations of over fifteen hundred suspected homosexuals, resulting in ruined lives, suicide and prison sentences up to life.

He realized with a sick heart that this could bring his mentor the District Attorney down, too. The opposition would use anything to smear his boss, and he could see the D.A.'s judgment being called into question for employing a homosexual and encouraging Paul's rising star. Every photo taken of them together would be employed in a campaign to oust the District Attorney. He knew the D.A.'s enemies were corrupt, if they got in power again the LAPD would have free reign to do whatever they wanted, just like the old days.

"So you just give in to them?"

"Have you asked yourself what this would do to your parents?" Paul's voice was sharp. "You know how religious they are. What's going to happen when they realize what we've been doing together?"

"They probably know already," David said wearily.

"It's different when it's in the papers, David. It's different when it's a scandal. You know how ugly they can get. It sucks everybody in. And it won't go away. It will be months and months of screaming headlines. You know what your mom and dad are like. It will destroy them. And it won't end with me. There will be witch hunts in the D.A's Office for others like us, then in the police department, in every branch of government. The press will demand it and nobody will be able to stop it until everybody gets burned."

David stood in front of him and shook his head. "And if you give them what they want? Do you really think that once they get their hands on those documents they're going to let any of us live?" he demanded caustically. "You have to expose them, you've got to give those documents to that reporter, Paul. It's the only way."

Paul put his face in his hands. "At least if I do as they say there's a chance this will all go away."

David crouched on the floor and took Paul's hands in his, imploring. "Think about what you're doing. They've committed murder, Paul. They've killed people and they'll kill more. They'll get away with all of it if you don't stand up. You're the only one who can do it. What has your whole life been for if not to stop people like this?"

He didn't have an answer. He didn't know anymore. He had to think. If only he could think. He pulled his hands from David's and looked at his watch. Two hours. It would take nearly an hour to get downtown to his office. Like a battered old man, he rose from the couch and went toward the front door.

"What are you going to do?"

Paul hesitated, looking back at David. "I don't know," he admitted. "I put the papers in my safe at work. I'm going to go get them."

David rose to his feet. "And then what?"

Paul stood with his hand on the doorknob, not saying anything, eyes fixed on the floor.

"If you give those documents to them," David said, his voice suddenly fierce, "I won't be here when you get back." He shook his head but his gaze never wavered from Paul's face. "There are some things I can forgive, but not this."

He stared at David helplessly, unable to speak, then went out the door without giving him an answer.

Paul got in his car, slamming the door, and lost control of himself. He pounded his fists furiously against the steering wheel until they hurt. He felt bombarded by such a rush of conflicting emotions he couldn't think straight, but cold anger quickly edged out fear and confusion in his mind. How could Jim Blake have done this to him? How could he have done it? He felt as if he had a noose around his neck and Blake had pulled it tight and sprung the trap door. Finally exhausted, his flailing fists stinging, he quieted down, resting his head in his arms, which were slung across the steering wheel.

What was he going to do about the documents? He didn't know. He kept thinking about David and what he'd said and the terrible look of hurt on his face. It was a look he never wanted to see again. As Paul's head lay in his arms, his eyes fell upon the outside rear view mirror and he jolted. Parked two cars behind him—David's dumpy Chevrolet, which had been handed down from his parents when they got a new car, was between them—a Buick rested at the curb with two men sitting inside. In the dimness of the evening he didn't recognize the car and it was too dark inside to see their faces. They could have been anybody, friends of one of the inhabitants of his building waiting to pick them up, but an alarm went off in his head. Were they here to follow him? There was only one way to find out.

He keyed the ignition and put the car in gear, pulling a U-turn across the coral tree lined median and heading east on San Vicente. He drove slowly, waiting for them to follow, but they didn't. Maybe he was just getting paranoid, he decided, but he kept checking the rear view mirror just in case.

Paul hardly noticed the road as he drove. The turmoil in his head calmed and he began to feel more like himself again. He knew in his gut David was right. It was so like David to instinctively know the right thing to do. It couldn't be any other way. He had struggled to live a life of integrity and to do the right thing, it was why he had become a lawyer and why he had become a prosecutor. It was the reason he had wanted to climb the ladder of success to become a district attorney in one of the most corrupt cities in the country. He couldn't betray who he was, whatever the price he had to pay. He knew he didn't always live up to his own ideals, but he also knew he couldn't let himself ever disappoint David like that again.

He would pick up the documents at his office and he would take them to Marvin Botwinick, and he would bring these people down and expose them for what they were, and if they used what they had to bring him down also, then so be it.

A kind of defiant relief came over him once he accepted what he was going to do. Everything might be taken away, all the work he had done, all the dreams gone. And what would be left for him in the void?

He wouldn't have to lie anymore.

It was such a little thing to have left, and yet the thought of it filled him with a lightness that he had never experienced before, and for the first time in his life he wondered if it might be worth it. To lose everything so that you never had to lie about yourself ever again.

And then he realized it was unfair to say he would lose everything. Whether there was prison time in his future or not, David would be waiting for him, and he felt such a rush of strength inside him that his eyes filled with tears. Because one thing he knew with certainty, above everything else, was that if he did the right thing, David would be there for him no matter how long it took, no matter how long he had to wait. That the world could strip him of almost everything and still he would have what mattered most. They could take away his career and destroy his reputation, but they couldn't take his integrity and they couldn't stop him from loving; only he could do that.

Paul had driven several blocks before he knew something was wrong. He heard the knocking first and then felt the back of the Fairlane begin to throb. He pulled to the curb on San Vicente just before it hit Wilshire and got out of the car. The back driver's side tire was bulging, half flat. He bent to examine the tread and it didn't take him long to find the head of a nail in the rubber.

He locked the car and began to walk back to the house. He went at a deliberate pace, but he wasn't in a hurry. There was no deadline to meet anymore, and he had enough time to get the documents to Botwinick later this evening. He'd have to borrow David's car. As he waited at a stoplight, the coincidence of having a flat tire now of all times settled uneasily upon him, and he thought again of the nail puncturing the rubber and what the odds were of that happening by accident. The light changed, and as he crossed the street, he recalled the moment before Pritchard Sondergaard hung up, the moment when he seemed to be weighing his options if Paul reneged on their agreement. Then he remembered the men sitting in the car in front of his apartment, waiting. Suddenly he felt ice cold to his core.

He began to run.

The telephone was ringing when he came in the door.

"David?" Paul called. "David?" He hesitated a moment when he received no reply. He let the phone ring and proceeded swiftly past the kitchen, glancing into the nook, and then down the hall into the bedroom. He had seen David's Chevy parked outside, so if he wasn't here, he couldn't have gone far. Unless. Unless the Buick with the two men in it had been waiting all along for an additional bargaining chip in case Paul went back on his promise. Their car had been gone from the front of the building when he'd returned, and with growing fear he surmised what they had done after he'd driven away.

"David? David, are you here?" He poked his head in the bathroom. No one was there. He ran back into the living room.

Rage gripped him as he grabbed the receiver and shouted into the phone, "Where is he?"

He heard the calm voice of Pritchard Sondergaard. "We thought you might need a little encouragement. Bring us what we want, and we'll give you what you want. Ten-thirty. The observatory at Griffith Park. Be there on the dot or he dies." The line went dead.

As Paul laid the receiver in its cradle, he asked himself if he should call the police. No, he couldn't risk it. Not when David's life was at stake. As far as he knew, the men who had taken David were Falk and Vincent—or their comrades in the LAPD. He had to do this himself.

Paul strode into his bedroom and threw open the closet door. He took a box from the back of a high shelf and brought it over to the bed. Crouching down on his knee, he pulled off the lid and took out the Smith & Wesson that lay inside. It was his father's pistol, and as the only son, it had gone to Paul upon his father's death. He hadn't fired it since he was a kid, but he had been a good shot, the best in his age category, and he gripped the handle with confidence. He loaded the gun with bullets then went to look for the keys to David's car.

◇◇◇

He had sped all the way downtown to his office, running red lights, passing other cars like a madman. Maybe when the super highways were complete, it would be a quick jaunt across town, but it was later than he wanted it to be when he'd finally opened his safe and took out the Department of Transportation documents.

Now they lay on the seat beside him as he headed north on Olive. He had the documents, but there wasn't going to be any trade-off. The fact that they had David didn't change that. David had been right. They had killed before and they would kill again. Giving in to them wouldn't set Paul or David free; it wouldn't solve anything. They would never be free until all the conspirators were rotting in prison or dead.

The downtown streets were nearly deserted at this hour on a Sunday night, most of the shops closed. In the distance he saw the glow of the Biltmore Hotel.

He checked his watch. He no longer had enough time to take the documents to Marvin Botwinick in Culver City, not if he was going to get to Griffith Park before his adversaries. He had no idea what he was going to encounter there, but the Smith & Wesson lay on the seat beside him and he knew he would use it if he had to. But he also knew he had to get the evidence to the reporter, so that no matter what happened that night in Griffith Park, the conspiracy would be exposed.

He searched his head for who he could get to deliver the documents to Botwinick, but nobody came to mind. None of his friends lived close enough, and he couldn't think of any messenger service he could quickly access this late on a Sunday night.

As he passed Pershing Square, an idea occurred to him and he reached in his pocket to make sure he had enough money for cab fare. Plucking bills from his wallet, he came across the note he had written down this afternoon, the cross streets where Jim Blake had wanted to meet him. He told himself none of that mattered anymore, and stuffed the wallet back in his pocket. After he pulled to the curb and got out of the car, his eyes scanned the park. It was dark, the lights only dimly illuminating the walkways, but he knew the subject of his search wouldn't be difficult to spot.

Sure enough, he was there, swathed in his red turban, sitting on a park bench.

Beatrice O'Conner, the middle-aged woman behind the ticket counter at the train station had a funny feeling about the young woman with curly brown hair buying a single one-way ticket to Spokane. She seemed oddly familiar, and yet Beatrice just couldn't place her. Someone who had gone to school with one of her children, perhaps? No, this girl had such a pretty face, she would have remembered. The movies, maybe? No, this girl just didn't have that glamorous movie star look. Pretty, but mousy. Perhaps she worked in one of the department stores where Beatrice shopped....

"That will be twenty-four dollars and fifty cents."

The young woman pushed the glasses down her nose and came up with the cash from her purse.

"A one-way ticket from L.A. to Spokane, Washington," Beatrice said. She slid the ticket across the counter.

"Thank you."

211

The voice was familiar, too, but still Beatrice couldn't place her.

The woman took the ticket, glanced over her shoulder, then did a double take. There was a colored girl with a suitcase standing on the platform looking at them, as if she was waiting to be noticed. When the girl realized she'd been spotted, a big grin spread across her face. Beatrice didn't like the colored very much, but she had to admit, when this girl smiled, she was awfully pretty and her face resonated with warmth.

The young woman at the counter dug into her purse, pulling out more bills, and Beatrice couldn't be sure because of the woman's glasses, but she thought there were joyful tears in her eyes.

"Make that two," the young woman said. "Make that two one-way tickets to Spokane."

Marvin Botwinick was typing like a maniac on a Smith Corona in his den when he heard a knock at the door. He didn't respond at first because when he was on a roll he got into a rhythm and found it impossible to stop until a train of thought had run its course. There was a beauty to it, like a classical pianist refusing to relinquish the keys until the piece was done. Finishing the page, he pulled it from the platen and laid it on top of several others. He had nearly completed the story. He knew it was powerful and filled with outrage and would blow the city sky high.

He went down the hall and passed the kids sitting on the living room rug up close to the television set. "I thought I told you to go to bed after *The Ed Sullivan Show*," he said. "And don't sit so close to the screen. Do you want to glow in the dark?"

He glanced back into the kitchen and spotted Julie finishing up with the dishes and listening to the radio. She probably hadn't heard the knock. He parted the gauzy curtain over the window in the front door. He had expected to see Paul Winters. To his surprise, there was a little colored woman standing on his porch. Waiting at the curb was a yellow cab. He opened the door and tilted his head, looking at her quizzically. It took a moment for him to realize the red-turbaned figure before him dressed in flowing flower-print garb was actually a young man. He was holding a stack of papers at his chest in his long thin arms.

"I believe you've been waiting for these?" he asked primly.

"Uh, um, yes," Botwinick said, taking the documents in his hands. "Could you, uh, wait here a moment while I look them over?" He hesitated, then said, "Would you like to come inside?"

The man on the porch shook his head.

"Could you wait here, then? I'll be right back," Marvin said. He brought the pile of documents to the dining room table and quickly went over them. Paul Winters had tagged the important documents with explanations of how they fit in the conspiracy. It was all here. All of it. All the proof he needed to back up his story and convince his editor.

He went back to the front door to thank the stranger, but no one was there. The cab had disappeared. He looked both ways on the long porch that fronted his Craftsman house, then walked down the flagstone path to the street. No one was out, and the street was quiet.

Whoever he was, the young man was gone.

Chapter 14

A blanket of darkness had fallen over Griffith Park. Paul turned north from Los Feliz Boulevard and sped through the residential streets leading to the park entrance, passing expensive homes shrouded in creeping blood-red bougainvillea and monstrously twisting trees that threw deep shadows everywhere. Streetlights along the route glowed but offered little light.

The road was deserted, the neighborhood silent, his headlights cutting the darkness as the blacktop began its gentle curve around the jutting steep promontory upon which the observatory perched above the city. He knew the observatory closed earlier in the evening. Nobody else would be there.

He looked at his watch again. He'd wanted to arrive before they did, to survey the situation, and to figure out a plan. Of course, he had no idea if they were thinking the same thing.

The road got darker, the houses forgotten and left behind, and only scrub and straggly pines covered the hillside. He continued to climb until there was nothing but the headlights grazing the road surrounded by night.

He cut the lights as the Chevy entered a short concrete tunnel near the top. When he came out the other end, he slowed the car and parked it on the side of the winding road behind some underbrush. In the moonlight he could see the blacktop curving up to the flat crest of the hill. From his viewpoint, he was too low to see the long parking area that led to the observatory, which hugged the far edge of the hilltop, a sentinel overlooking the city.

The air was chilly, and the only sound was the gentle wind in the trees and the echoes of his steps. As he made his way up the road, he heard the hum of a car engine in the distance and ducked into the undergrowth and pine dotted slope at the edge of the shoulder. He hunkered down there, waiting until the interior of the tunnel glowed and then headlights flashed in his eyes as an automobile took the curve out of the tunnel and sped past him up the incline leading to the parking lot in front of the observatory. He was pretty sure it was the Buick he'd spotted in front of his apartment.

All he could think about was that David was in that car, and instinctively he laid his hand on the pistol in his pocket. He made his way quickly along the slope, the foliage providing cover, peering over the edge now and then to observe that the car had come to a halt in the middle of the vast empty lot. Beyond it, he could see the three black domes of the observatory rising against the cobalt blue night sky. Lights had come on in the city and there were more stars strewn across the valley below than in the sky above.

Leaving the headlights on, somebody got out of the driver's door and stood beside the car. Paul couldn't be sure, but he thought it was Falk. The windows were dark and he couldn't see anyone inside. He wondered who else was in the car. Vincent, in the passenger seat? Most likely. That meant David was probably alone in the back. For a brief moment he feared that they had broken their promise as he had, and the two cops had come alone, that they had already done away with David. But no, they wouldn't risk it. They only increased their chance of exposure by doing anything until the Department of Transportation documents were safely in their hands.

As he continued along the slope, trying to get a better view, he heard an oddly familiar murmur and stopped to listen. Someone was there, in the bushes, using the cover of darkness as he was, but for a very different purpose. Silently as he could, grabbing onto branches to keep from sliding down the hill, he made his way toward the sounds.

In a few moments he came upon two men, one leaning against a tree, his pants at his ankles, the other on his knees before him, both wrapped in shadows. They were startled when they heard him, jolting into standing position. He couldn't make out their faces, but he knew they were scared.

He held up his I.D. in his wallet as if it were a badge. "LAPD," he whispered. "Give me your identification."

The two men did as instructed, and even though he couldn't make out their names from their driver's licenses in the dimness, he studied them as if he could. "You're going to help me," he said, "do you understand?"

The two men, terrified, nodded mutely.

He handed back their wallets. "I want you to climb around to the opposite side of the hill. I want you to do it quickly. Make sure you're not seen by the people in the car parked up there. Then I want you to gather some stones." He looked at his watch. "It's ten-oh-five. In exactly ten minutes, I want you to toss those stones onto the parking lot pavement. I want them to hit the edge of the lot over there, do you understand? Then I want you to get out of here. I want you to run down the hill and don't come back."

They nodded and Paul waved at them to go. They disappeared almost immediately and in a moment he couldn't hear them anymore as they traversed the hill. He climbed to the edge of the pavement and waited.

He was sure now the man standing beside the car was Falk. A red ember glowed in his hand, and occasionally he brought it to his lips and took a drag. The lieutenant's eyes were trained on the road leading up to the parking lot, waiting for Paul to drive up.

Falk almost jumped when the first stone landed at the far side of the parking lot. He dropped his cigarette and went for his Remington. He said something in a muffled voice into the window, then rounded the hood of the car and set off toward the sound to investigate. Vincent got out of the front passenger door and followed him, his gun drawn. A couple more stones rained down at the edge of the blacktop and then there was silence. In his head Paul pictured the two frightened men on the slope slip-sliding and running for their lives.

Seeing the car there, unattended, its headlights splashing oblong circles on the blacktop, Paul formed a makeshift plan.

He slipped off his shoes and made a run for it toward the car, always keeping it positioned in a straight line between him and the two cops on the other side of it so they couldn't spot him. He approached the car silently, quelling his ragged breath, and crouched down beside the back driver's side wheel. He was about to peek in the rear window and alert David to his presence, when he heard the back door on the other side of the car open. What was going on? Why was David getting out of the car? To make a run for it? That dashed one of his possible plans of escape: jumping in the front seat, and if the keys were in the ignition, simply flooring the car and speeding away.

And then, to his utter surprise, he realized the man getting out of the back seat wasn't David after all. A white fedora hovered beside the roof of the car. But what the hell was Pritchard Sondergaard doing here? To make sure the promised return of the documents went without a hitch? To

217

make sure the papers were complete? No, Paul reasoned, the meeting was set up in this out-of-the-way place to take down those who knew about the conspiracy. And Falk and Vincent hardly needed Sondergaard to supervise their killings. Then another possibility struck him and he knew how desperate the situation had become. He had seen it before in organized crime, when everything started crashing down and the only way out was killing all the witnesses—including other accomplices—and that meant the conspiracy was beginning to feed on itself, and Sondergaard had undoubtedly gone from an instigator to the next victim.

"Get back in the car!" Falk ordered from the far side of the parking lot, waving his Remington.

"I am not," Sondergaard said huffily, "accustomed to taking orders from the likes of you."

Apparently the two cops had satisfied their curiosity regarding the noises at the edge of the parking lot, because they strode back toward the car, Falk in the lead, their guns still raised.

Paul peeked over the trunk of the car to see Falk approach Sondergaard, who stood with the arrogant stance of a little man who has known power. While Vincent held back and observed, the lieutenant pistol-whipped the lawyer across the face. "This is all your mess," he growled, "and our friends aren't happy about it." He took Sondergaard—who began to whimper—by the collar and dragged him around the Buick toward the trunk. Paul crouched lower and made his way to the front of the car.

"Stop it!" Sondergaard cried. "You will not touch me!" And then his voice lost its characteristic haughtiness, and he begged, "Please... no... please..."

The trunk popped open, and Paul knew what was going to happen next. He ducked down and looked under the car. He heard a gunshot and then Sondergaard's corpulent body

218

falling heavily into the trunk. He could only see Falk's feet now, and then the white linen hat tumbled to the ground beside Falk's shoes and came to rest there.

Paul clung to the grille, shaken by the brutality of the murder, and wondered frantically what he was going to do now. If David was in the car, that was one thing. If not, he had to find some way to get out of here. Maybe just make a run for it before they decided to drive off. He inched his head up; the inside of the car was dark and he couldn't see through the windshield. Had they brought David or not?

Falk slammed the trunk lid and he and Vincent rounded their respective sides of the car. Paul had to do something. He couldn't let them drive away if David was still in the back seat.

He jumped out from the front of the Buick, shooting twice, at Falk directly in front of him, and at Vincent reaching for the front passenger door. Then he dove back for cover directly in front of the hood as shots rang out around him. He heard the doors on each side of the car open and slam shut, and when the Buick engine revved, he knew he was in trouble. He somersaulted out of the way as the car lurched forward and skidded off across the blacktop, laying rubber in its wake.

Down on all fours, he watched as the car slowed to a crawl a hundred feet away and the driver's window rolled open. Falk aimed his gun and shot a few stray bullets his way, which ricocheted on the pavement around him. Paul crouched in firing stance but resisted returning fire in case David was in the car. Suddenly the back door on the far side of the Buick was flung open and David sprang out toppling to the ground. He quickly recovered and found his feet and bounded toward the edge of the parking lot with all his might.

The Buick swerved and headed after him.

David got halfway to the pine trees peeking over the edge of the slope and then a shot rang out and David seemed to freeze, his arms reaching up to the night sky, and then he collapsed and crumpled into a heap on the ground.

Paul heard a cry of anguish from his own throat, "*No!*"

The Buick screeched to a stop beside the fallen figure and Vincent jumped out and dragged David toward the back of the car. As Paul began sprinting toward them the trunk popped open and Vincent heaved David's slumped body into the trunk on top of Sondergaard's bloody corpse and slammed the lid shut.

Before Paul could reach them Vincent was back in the passenger seat and the Buick careened off, heading for the road leading down the hill.

Paul raced after them until he thought his lungs would burst, his heart a pile driver in his chest, each gulp of oxygen like shards of ice down his throat. His eyes filled with tears and his vision blurred as the two red taillights became three and four, and then slipped from view as the Buick shot down the hill and disappeared through the tunnel where Paul had left his car.

Suddenly he was utterly alone in the night, running with every ounce of strength he had left, the only sounds the slap of his stockinged footfalls and the beat of his heart and the rasp of his breath, which seemed to pound the words through his head again and again, *He could be alive, he could still be alive, David could still be alive.* The ache in his heart was so deep he didn't think he would survive if it weren't true.

He staggered to the Chevy, collapsed inside, turned the ignition and wheeled the car around and headed through the tunnel and down the hill. The car roared along the curving road heedless of bumps and potholes. At first there was only darkness ahead, and then as the car jounced over the pavement at breakneck speed, he caught sight of the red beads of taillights in the distance.

He pushed the gas pedal to the floor as the Chevy swerved and he fought to keep control of the steering wheel. He passed a stop sign without stopping. They were in the residential area now at the foot of the park, houses flipping past him like cards in a deck, heading toward the stoplight at the intersection at Los Feliz Boulevard.

Ahead of him Paul could see the light turn from yellow to red as the Buick sailed through the intersection and down Vermont. He tried to follow but cross-traffic on Los Feliz had already entered the intersection and he slammed on his brakes, the car fishtailing to a screaming halt. Passing cars angrily blared their horns at him.

He yanked on the emergency brake and jumped out of the car, hoisting himself up with one hand on the open door, the other on the roof, straining his neck to keep sight of the Buick as it slipped away down Vermont. He watched in anguish as the red taillights quickly receded in the distance and vanished in the night.

When they freed him from his interrogation room, and he'd seen the open door to interrogation room three—and no one inside—a dark hollow of rage and loss opened inside him and Blake knew he'd made the most terrible mistake of his life. He felt as if they had found a way to cut out his soul and only a shell of him remained. And all he could think about was that somehow he had to warn Paul Winters, if it wasn't already too late.

They had given his gun and badge back—as if nothing had happened—and Dr. Stone had told him his job was safe, in fact he'd be transferred immediately to the robbery division, and that the doctor wanted to start seeing him

221

three times a week. When Stone smiled at him, that fond sympathetic smile, he'd shoved the doctor against a wall and walked out.

He went directly to the pay phone in the main corridor of the jail and dropped coins in the slot to call Paul. The phone rang and rang but nobody answered. An unbearable weight of guilt hung upon him as he replaced the receiver. He didn't know how he could ever face Paul Winters again. How could Paul ever forgive him? How could he ever forgive himself? He felt bereft. When it had counted most, he had caved in, he'd let them manipulate him into destroying someone he cared about; he'd been a coward and they'd made him sing. He felt so agitated he couldn't stand it.

Nothing he could do could ever make up for what he had done.

A young uniformed officer brought him back to his car, which sat where he had left it that morning adjacent to the construction site. But instead of getting in his car, he had waited until the officer was out of sight, then strode to the pay phone at the gas station down the block to try to reach Paul again. After incessant rings, he dropped the receiver in its cradle.

For a moment he didn't know what to do with himself. Then like a ghost returning to the last place he had known before death, Blake gravitated toward the high fence surrounding the freeway construction area.

He hoisted himself up on the fence then climbed over. Nothing had changed since this morning, and he could see the temporary tool sheds and big trucks and the piles of sand and gravel and dirt in the moonlight. But it was the newly poured concrete that interested him.

He had just begun to walk toward it when he heard a car pull up to a gate beyond a tin tool shed, and the clink of someone working a padlock. Blake melted into the shadows. A moment later a Buick entered the site and drove to the spot where concrete had last been poured. Leaving the headlights on, two dark figures got out of the car.

"Get the shovels from the shed," one ordered.

It was too dark to see the face of the man who spoke—though the headlights laid a swath of light in the dirt at the edge of the new concrete, the rest of the construction site was shrouded in darkness—but Blake recognized the voice. It was Lieutenant Falk, who went to the back of the car while Vincent headed for the tool shed.

Blake watched from the distance as Falk opened the trunk. In the dim red glow from the taillights he could see a man sprawled out on top of something white. It took him a moment to realize the figure was lying on top of the bloody body of Pritchard Sondergaard, almost glowing in his white linen suit. It took another moment to recognize who the man was. With a jolt he knew he had seen him before, Saturday afternoon. He was the handsome young man Paul had kissed. David. The man Paul Winters was in love with. At first he couldn't fathom why David could possibly be here, about to be buried in a nameless grave, and then it struck him that what he had done in that interrogation room might have caused the world to go terribly wrong in ways he couldn't have imagined.

When Falk went to the front of the car, Blake spotted movement in the trunk. David curled into fetal position and then was still again.

Blake sank deeper into the shadows and waited to make his move.

Paul sped down Vermont trying to catch sight of the Buick. His heart would leap when he spotted a car that looked like it, only to find it was another make driven by a middle-aged couple who looked frightened when he pulled up beside them and peered into their windows. He began to fear he'd lost them forever.

He was overcome with despair, and yet he didn't give up hope. David could still be alive. Paul had lost them, but he could find them before it was too late if only he could figure out where they had gone.

Where could they be taking him?

The only answer he could come up with was: they were taking him where they took all the others. Bullock. O'Keife. Hollings. Where they would have taken Victoria Lynn if they could have found her.

But where?

He wracked his brain to try to figure out the location they had used to bury all their victims. It was the one question he had never been able to answer. Far off in the desert? It was possible, but he didn't think so. But how could you get away with burying several bodies in the city? Where could you do it without fear of witnesses? Without fear some sniffing dog would come across the grave and raise suspicion?

Paul searched his mind frantically, trying to figure out where that could possibly be. Something he had forgotten earlier in the day came back to him. The message Jim Blake had left with David and the cross streets south of downtown. He envisioned the gas station and the shabby houses he had passed earlier that day, but he couldn't understand their significance. And then he remembered what was across the street.

He floored the car and headed for downtown. Traffic was sparse and he coasted through red lights when the intersections were clear and gunned it the rest of the way. He only paused unnecessarily one time: as he crossed an already completed overpass downtown above the new freeway construction, he found himself unconsciously putting his foot on the brake.

He looked down upon the vast expanse of concrete below, a pale flat ribbon snaking from downtown that would eventually stretch to the sea, miles and miles of gray turned silver in the moonlight, and, sick to his stomach, he understood what Jim Blake had tried to tell him and he knew without a doubt where all the bodies were buried.

Lieutenant Falk thought he heard something by the tool shed and pulled out his Remington. As he began to walk in that direction to investigate, his gun raised, Vincent came out of the shack.

"What's the matter?"

"I thought I heard something."

"It was just me, clanging around in there. C'mon, let's get this done."

Hesitating, Falk scanned the darkness, then shrugged. He stripped off his jacket and laid his pistol on top of it on the roof of the car. He gently touched the spot of blood on his shoulder.

"Did he hit you?"

"It's just a graze." He took the offered shovel and led Vincent to a patch of dirt glowing in the headlights and said, "Here. They'll pave over this spot tomorrow."

Vincent was about to plant his shovel in the dirt when a sound came from the open trunk. A moan.

Falk sighed. "Take care of it."

Setting his shovel aside, Vincent drew his gun. He made his way around the car to the trunk.

Falk took a bite of earth with his shovel. "Find something to muffle the sound," he called after him.

David lay in the trunk with his head lolling. He let out another low moan. Vincent stood above him a moment then put his pistol to David's head. Just then he felt cold steel at the back of his neck.

At the front of the car Falk heard the gunshot and gritted his teeth. "I told you to be quiet about it!" he hissed. When he didn't get any response, he tilted his head, puzzled. "Vincent?" He buried the shovel in a pile of dirt and angrily stomped his way around the Buick. Before it registered that his gun was no longer lying on the roof where he'd left it, he was already at the back of the car. He stopped in his tracks. Vincent lay on the ground in a pool of blood. Falk's shoe kicked something and he looked down and spotted his own Remington on the ground at his feet. He looked at it curiously then bent down to pick it up; he stopped when he realized it had just been fired. Then a figure that had been crouching and hiding stepped out from the far side of the car. Falk saw the glint of Vincent's gun and who was holding it before a flash of light exploded in his face.

◇◇◇

Paul heard the second shot as he scrambled over the fence. He landed on the ground on all fours, the Smith & Wesson tumbling onto the dirt beside him. He crouched there frozen in place, waiting for another sound, but none came.

Slowly he got up, collecting the pistol, and moved cautiously around a tin tool shed, hugging the side of the structure. A siren began to wail in the distance. A nearby cruiser had heard the gunshots or a neighbor had seen intruders in the construction site and called the police. Ahead of him, the Buick came into view, headlights blazing, the trunk open. It took him a moment to see the two figures slumped on the ground lit by the red taillights. He didn't have to look closely to know both of them were dead, their guns lying beside them. It appeared Falk and Vincent had got in an argument and shot one another.

He strode to the trunk trying to quiet the hysteria rising in him and crouched over David, who lay perfectly still, his back to Paul, curled in a ball on top of the bloody mess that was the remains of Pritchard Sondergaard.

"David? David, can you hear me?"

There was no response. Paul quickly checked his vital signs. His heart was beating rapidly, his breath was as feeble as a frayed thread. Paul found a wet bullet hole in his lower back, and pressed his right hand firmly over it even though it was leaking little blood. With his left hand, he reached over and held David's hand; he thought David returned the pressure.

"David?"

The siren grew to a shrill scream and flashing lights appeared on the other side of the fence. A moment later a patrol car came through the gate to the construction site and the siren died out. A lone uniformed officer got out and stared, his mouth gaping open, as if trying to absorb the carnage before him.

"We need an ambulance," Paul shouted to him. "We have a gunshot victim here!" The officer ducked back into the cruiser momentarily to make the call.

Paul held David's hand tighter. "Don't go," he said, his voice a strangled whisper. "Please, David, hang on. I love you, I really love you." And then he buried his face in David's shoulder and began to cry, deep heaving sobs that shook his body. He couldn't be sure, but he thought David's hand tightened its tentative hold on his.

Then Paul heard something close by in the darkness and he raised his head in alarm. Someone was out there. His first instinct was fear, but just as quickly it dawned on him that it wasn't a sound he'd heard, but silence.

The silence of someone listening.

And then, ever so quietly, he heard the echo of footsteps receding into the night.

Chapter 15

The massive iron front gates of the 1920s Spanish-style residency hotel on Franklin opened onto a quiet courtyard of palms and sweet honeysuckle. The Santa Anas of the week before had given way to a heavy overcast sky and sticky morning drizzle; Paul sidestepped puddles as he followed the wide flagstone path to the front door. After getting directions from the man at the front desk, Paul took the stairs to the second floor and knocked at a door at the end of the hall. The chirp of birds came from inside.

He heard a drawer closing and then the door opened. Jim Blake seemed surprised to see him. He stared for the briefest moment, lowered his eyes, then held the door further open and waved Paul inside. The room's single window was open and a breeze played in the curtains. A suitcase was open on the bed, clothes folded neatly inside. A drawer in the bureau had been pulled open, the contents, socks and underwear and T-shirts, not yet packed. In a corner by the window on the only chair in the room sat a bird cage fluttering with canaries.

"I'd ask you to sit down, but…"

"That's all right." They stood there awkwardly for a moment; Blake seemed to have a hard time looking him in the eye. Paul noticed a folded newspaper on the bed, with its banner headlines breathlessly reporting the scandal: the arrests of seven city council members on murder and graft charges, the shootout with police on Sunset Boulevard that left the gangster Mel Fischer dead, the apparent fallout between Falk and Vincent that left them both corpses bathed in their own blood, the recovery under the newly paved freeway of the bodies of those who had discovered the conspiracy and not lived to tell. Paul had gone personally to inform Mrs. O'Keife of her husband's death, one of the hardest things he'd ever done.

"I don't know if you heard," Paul said, "but Lieutenant Falk's badge and I.D. weren't found on his body." He paused, then added, "Odd thing is, later that night somebody used them to check a file out of the evidence room. The officer behind the desk was so drunk he doesn't even remember handing out the file. I believe a negative and a photograph were inside. No one has seen them since."

"Fancy that," Blake said.

Paul thought he might have seen a smile flicker on his lips, but then they straightened to a bitter line.

"There's still my confession."

"Strangely, that seems to have disappeared, too." A call to Jeff Dupuis had taken care of that. It turned out the janitors he took cigarette breaks with had a master key to every office in the jail. He glanced over at the bird cage in the corner. "I wouldn't take you for someone who kept birds."

"I'm not really. When they started raiding businesses Pritchard Sondergaard owned downtown looking for evidence of his part in the conspiracy, it turned out he was the owner of the bar where I made the arrest Thursday night."

Paul remembered David had told him that the lawyer was rumored to own a bar downtown among his real estate holdings.

Blake went to the bureau and took the socks from the drawer. "I dropped by yesterday. They were closing the place down, confiscating papers in the back office, but they didn't seem to know what to do about the birds." He laid the socks in the suitcase, and finally looked at Paul directly. "The first thing Charlie Turner said to me was what a shame it was that they were stuck in that smoky bar. I don't know, I just couldn't leave them there." He glanced back at the cage on the chair. "And now I don't think they'll let me take them on the train."

"So you're leaving?"

"I thought I'd go back," Blake said, avoiding Paul's gaze. "I'm not sure why I came in the first place. I don't know what I was looking for." He went back to the drawer, lifted out a stack of neatly folded T-shirts and underwear and laid them on top of the bureau. There was only one thing left at the bottom of the drawer. A five-by-seven photograph in a cardboard frame.

Paul took a step toward him. "You've got to forget what happened in that little room. I have."

Blake laid his big hands on the edge of the bureau as if he didn't have the strength to stand on his own, his shoulders sagging, his head hanging low. "Why did you come? Why couldn't you just leave it alone?"

"I wanted to thank you."

Blake turned his face to him, and there were tears in his eyes, but anger, too. "After what I did to you?"

"You gave me the most important thing in my life. I can never repay you for that. I know what you did for us. I know what you did for David."

Swallowing thickly, Blake asked, "How is he?"

"He's going to be okay," Paul said quietly. "We were lucky. The bullet didn't hit any vital organs. It went straight through. He's getting out of the hospital tomorrow."

Angling his head toward the bird cage, Blake said, "Maybe he'd like to have them."

Paul thought a moment. "You know, I think they'd be really good for David during his recovery." He chuckled softly. "If I know David, he'll be bringing them outside every day to get some sun and letting them fly free in the apartment."

"I think Charlie Turner would have liked that."

Paul came forward toward Blake until they were face to face. A curl of his black hair had fallen forward, and Paul reached up and gently brushed the lock back from his forehead.

"Take care of yourself, Jim."

As he passed the bureau to pick up the bird cage by the window, Paul saw the photo in the drawer was of a young handsome man in his Navy uniform. Proud, so full of hope, like a thousand other pictures he had seen. He picked up the cage, sending the canaries into a chirping frenzy. When he turned to go back around the bed, he saw Blake was sitting on it beside the suitcase with the photograph in his hands, gazing down at it in his lap.

Paul stopped in front of him and set down the cage on the floor.

"Forgive him and forgive yourself. It's the only thing that's going to get you through." He put his hand on Blake's shoulder. "You loved him and he loved you. It's something you should cherish. They took everything else. Don't let them take that."

Blake just looked down at the picture as if he was lost in thought. Paul picked up the cage and went over to the door, but he didn't open it. He turned back and tilted his head.

"Did you quit already?"

Blake didn't look up from the photo. "I was going to hand in my resignation on the way to the train station."

Paul nodded slowly, then opened the door. He stopped again and looked back. "I hear the winters in Wisconsin

232

are brutal. Maybe you should stick around. I could use a friend in the LAPD. I don't have many."

When he didn't get a response, Paul hesitated a moment at the door, then silently he went out carrying the bird cage. Blake was still gazing down at the photograph in his hands when Paul closed the door behind him.

Acknowledgements

This book wouldn't have been possible without the extraordinary work of the following historians and memoirists: Jonathan Katz, *Gay American History*; John D'Emilio, *Sexual Politics, Sexual Communities*; Stuart Timmons, *The Trouble with Harry Hay*; Lillian Faderman and Stuart Timmons, *Gay L.A.*; Helen P. Branson and Will Fellows, *Gay Bar*; John Buntin, *L.A. Noir*. I thank you all.

A special thanks to Peter Cashorali, Eric A. Gordon, Daniel Harris and Jerry Rosen for help on this book.

2519274R00127

Made in the USA
San Bernardino, CA
01 May 2013